FIC
JAR

3 24891 0901493 3
Jaramillo, Ann.

La linea

PEIRCE ES
CHICAGO PUBLIC SCHOOLS

BY **ANN JARAMILLO**

la línea

SQUARE FISH

SQUARE
FISH

An Imprint of Macmillan

LA LÍNEA. Copyright © 2006 by Ann Jaramillo.
All rights reserved. Printed in the United States of America by R. R. Donnelley &
Sons Company, Harrisonburg, Virginia. For information, address Square Fish,
175 Fifth Avenue, New York, NY 10010.

Square Fish and the Square Fish logo are trademarks of Macmillan
and are used by Roaring Brook Press under license from Macmillan.

Library of Congress Cataloging-in-Publication Data
Jaramillo, Ann.
La línea / Ann E. Jaramillo.
p. cm.
"A Deborah Brodie Book."
Summary: When fifteen-year-old Miguel's time finally comes to leave his poor
Mexican village, cross the border illegally, and join his parents in California,
his younger sister's determination to join him soon imperils them both.

ISBN 978-0-312-37354-2

[1. Brothers and sisters—Fiction. 2. Emigration and immigration—Fiction.
3. Survival—Fiction. 4. Mexicans—Fiction. 5. Mexico—Fiction.]   I. Title.
PZ7.J28278Lin 2006
[Fic]—dc22
2005020133

Originally published in the United States by Roaring Brook Press
Square Fish logo designed by Filomena Tuosto
Designed by Patti Ratchford
First Square Fish Edition: July 2008
20 19 18 17 16 15 14 13 12 11
macteenbooks.com
AR: 4.3 / F&P: S / LEXILE: 650L

To Luis
Mi Querido

ACKNOWLEDGMENTS

Thank you to the individuals and organizations who work to bring to light the struggles of immigrants who come to this country. The Pew Hispanic Center in Washington, D.C., and The Center for Comparative Immigration Studies at the University of California–San Diego provided valuable background data and statistics.

The California Rural Legal Assistance Foundation's "Stop Gatekeeper" project highlights the abuses suffered by immigrants at the border. Series by the *Christian Science Monitor,* National Public Radio, and the *Los Angeles Times,* especially the moving reporting done by Sonia Nazario, put a human face on the data. Groups such as Humane Borders (to name just one) are out there every day, on the border, saving lives.

Deborah Brodie is my editor. She believed in *La Línea* and knew what to do with it. I'm pretty sure she's the best there is.

Fuertes abrazos to my English as a Second Language classes at La Paz Middle School who reviewed the manuscript. Your "thumbs up" and "thumbs down" helped me make the book reflect your experiences. You know who you are, and you are special.

Mil gracias a Cruz Reynoso, Adrian Andrade, and Irma Herrera. You used your precious time to read the book and offer comments. Your kind words mean a lot.

Many, many thanks to good friends Angélica López-Simons, Ruth Barraza, Alma Saucedo, and Cher Nicolas. You made sure I got it right, and I am grateful for your insights and suggestions.

Thank you to my family members who read too many versions of the manuscript but still continued to encourage me: Mom (Dorie), Petrea, Matthew, and Virginia. A special thank-you to Mateo, for believing in your mom every step of the way.

Most of all, thank you, Luis R., for saying again and again, "Good idea, Mom. Now go write it." I could never have written this book without you. —A. J.

CHAPTER 1

I should have known Elena would find a way to go north. If I'd kept my eyes open, if I'd been paying any attention at all, I might have seen what she was up to. After all, I'd dreamed about crossing *la línea* for years. Why should my sister be any different? But it was my fifteenth birthday, and Elena was the last thing on my mind.

I opened one eye and looked down at the wooden crate at the foot of my bed. Abuelita always left something for me to open, and I always knew what would be inside. *Calcetines, una camiseta, chones.* Something useful. Something my grandma could afford. Something I needed. Something I didn't want.

But there was nothing. No present. *Nada.* I rubbed my eyes and checked again. No, nothing. Not even the usual pair of underpants this year? Of course there was never enough money for a gift I didn't need. But any small thing would be okay. *Cualquier miseria.* I rolled over and covered my head with my blanket.

What I wanted was a pair of jeans, like the ones I saw Juanito wearing last week. They weren't like the pants I wore to work on the *rancho* every day, the knees patched and darned by Abuelita, frayed on the bottom. The jeans I wanted were bigger and looser and hung low. They got frayed because you let them drag on the ground and you stepped on them—on purpose, just because you could, because it didn't matter if they wore out or not.

But what I *really* wanted couldn't be wrapped up in a package. It cost thousands and thousands, and only Papá could give it to me. And he was thousands and thousands of kilometers away.

What could I remember about Papá? I thought I could remember sitting on his lap as he read aloud to me, when I was still little enough to sit on his lap. I liked the faint scent of his hair oil, the clove gum he chewed to cover up the cigarettes he smoked behind my mother's back. I liked the slow, careful way he pronounced each word, and how his moustache curved up when he read a line he enjoyed.

Abuelita made sure I didn't forget the important things about Papá. Every chance she got, she told the story of how he educated himself. He went to school only to the fourth grade. After that, the government closed *la primaria* in San Jacinto. He had to work on Abuelo's *rancho*, anyway, to help the family.

"He herded the goats and watered the corn with a book in one hand, and still he did more work than anyone else!" Abuelita always said. In those days, Papá could save a *peso* here and there. He used the money to buy books. The few he had, he read over and over until he knew long passages by heart.

I was the firstborn, so Papá should have named me Domingo, after himself and Abuelo and Bisabuelo and Tatarabuelo—and all the Cervantes as far back as anyone could remember. But Papá declared I wouldn't be like him, starting with his name. Miguel Carlos Octavio Pablo de Cervantes, he named me, after the authors he admired. Those were his saints, so those were the names I got.

And Papá proclaimed I would get an education. I would have a good, important job, one where I didn't have to break my back to put a few *frijoles y tortillas* on the table. *No quiero que sufras como yo*. That's how Papá put it.

I leaned over the side of my bed to pick up the pants I'd left on the floor the night before. On top of them lay a plain white envelope. Well, at least I got a card. I sighed. Abuelita loved me. She wished she could give me more. This year, there had been no money at all. It wasn't her fault.

But there was no card inside. No *Feliz Cumpleaños Nieto*. Instead, there was just a small folded note.

"It's been six years, eleven months, and twelve days since I left to go north across *la línea*. It's time for you to come. Go see Don Clemente. He'll help you." It was signed, simply, "Papá."

Papá had never written a note before. He'd never asked me to see Don Clemente before. And I didn't know until then that he'd counted each day since he left, that he numbered them one by one, just the way I did. I'd been waiting for this moment ever since I was eight. Could it be true this time, finally?

For once, I didn't care about a birthday present. If Papá's note was true, my real life was finally beginning. This was day number one.

CHAPTER 2

I picked up my soccer ball and twirled it on my index finger. It was scuffed and stained and the plastic insides bulged out in two places. Soccer was just a memory now. I hadn't made the cut for the best team, the one I had to get on if I wanted a chance to turn pro. I remembered *el sueño* I'd had just before waking. I knew the dream by heart. It was the same one I'd had a thousand times.

In my dream, when my turn came, I didn't go north to California. Instead, I played soccer for Cruz Azul or Chivas, America, or Necaxa. I was famous. I was very, very rich. I returned to San Jacinto in a shiny new black SUV, riding up high, around and around *la plaza,* looking down on the people. They looked back up at me, but they had no eyes, no noses, no mouths. I didn't know who anyone was.

I brought Mamá, Papá, and the twins back home. I built us a mansion, the biggest one in the whole state, ten times the size of Don Clemente's. I always woke up, in a cold sweat, just as I put the key in the door. I shook my head hard. Soccer was just a dream now, and a dead one. *Ya basta. Olvídalo.*

I heard Abuelita shuffling around our little kitchen. She'd been up before five and had already stoked the fire for breakfast. She talked quietly to herself as she moved about.

"*Ahora, las tortillas.* How many will Miguel want?" Abuelita mumbled. The *masa* slapped softly in her hands. "And Elena? *¡Sabrá Dios!*"

I looked over at my sister. She slept, curled up in a little ball, exhausted. Every night that she couldn't sleep—like last night, like most nights—Elena pulled Mamá's letters out of a little woven bag she kept under her bed. She read them, over and over, one by one, in chronological order.

In almost seven years, we'd seen Mamá just once, a little over three years ago, for three days. She'd slipped home for her sister's, Tía Consuelo's, funeral, using up all the saved money to pay a *coyote* to get her back across *la línea*.

Elena had to grow up without a mother, so she hoarded what she could of Mamá, her letters. The words were like little drops of water to a person dying of thirst—enough to give hope; not enough to make a difference.

I threw on my pants and shirt, tucked Papá's note in my pocket, and stepped quietly out of our room. Abuelita stood at the stove, spooning my birthday *pozole* into a bowl. I kissed her on top of her head. She touched my cheek and made the sign of the cross on my forehead.

Abuelita set the bowl on the table. "Eat, Miguel. Eat."

I took a handful of oregano out of a bowl, rubbed it in my palms, and watched it land on top of the steaming soup. Abuelita gave me two of her handmade *tortillas*. I tore one and dipped it into the *pozole*. The pungent *maíz* mingled with the smell of roasting chiles and the beginnings of *sopa*. One of our chickens had already been killed for dinner. Abuelita plucked the feathers from its lifeless body.

She turned her back to me. "Don Clemente has gone to *la capital*," she said quietly. "He won't be back until Sunday.

"I'll tell Elena the news if you want," Abuelita continued. "But it's better coming from you. She deserves to hear it from you."

"*Sí*, Abuelita." I said it respectfully. I sounded obedient.

I didn't want to be the one to tell Elena. She'd have one of her famous temper tantrums. She'd cry for hours. Nothing I could say would stop it—except to say I'd take her with me. And that was not going to happen.

Ten minutes later, Elena dragged herself out of bed and into the kitchen. She rubbed her eyes and yawned. She looked like she was three years old instead of thirteen.

I couldn't tell her. The words I needed to say felt like mud in my mouth. Abuelita let out a deep sigh, turned her back to me, and stirred the *frijoles* bubbling in the pot on the stove.

I walked out, barefoot, and stood at the edge of our *ranchito*. I dug my toes into the soft, dusty dirt and stared out at the corn-field. The stalks were dry, the cobs stunted and diseased. Every year, the drought got worse. We tried diverting the springwater. We'd carried water by hand. Nothing worked.

And even if our corn didn't die because of the drought, even if the corn grew tall and green with silky golden tassels, we couldn't sell it for more than a few *pesos*. Mexico was flooded with cheap foreign corn. Our market had dried up, along with *el maíz*.

If Papá and Mamá didn't send a little money every month, we would starve. Even if I wanted to, I couldn't help here anymore.

CHAPTER 3

Every year on my birthday, Chuy, Lalo, and I went up to the waterfall to swim. *Gracias a Dios* for my friends. I had to wait days for Don Clemente, and I'd go crazy if I stayed at home.

Halfway up the path that led into the hills, Chuy and Lalo sat lounging under the shade of the big tree. *"¡Apúrate!"* said Chuy.

He jumped up, pocketing the carving he was working on. "You're late."

Most of the springs had dried up, but we knew one secret place, far back in the hills and higher up. We climbed and climbed until we came to the narrow crevice in the cliff we'd discovered years before. We squeezed our bodies through and into the small gorge.

Our little waterfall had dwindled to a trickle, but the pool was there. It wasn't deep enough to dive into, so we stripped down to our underwear and floated in the clear blue water.

"Remember that time up here when we practiced farting?" Chuy asked. He stood up and demonstrated once, just to show he could still do it.

I laughed. "Yeah, we tortured Moreno real good. He never caught us, either. Our farts were quiet, but deadly."

Señor Moreno was our fifth-grade teacher. We'd hated him because he smelled like old onions and picked on Chuy for no good reason. We figured the *pedos* were at least self-defense against Moreno's bad breath.

"¿Y el año pasado?" I pointed at *mi amigo.* *"Tú,* Lalo. You got all that tequila and beer and dared us to drink it. Man, I thought I'd never quit throwing up."

Lalo didn't say anything, just smiled. He knew I wasn't mad. Up here, we felt hidden from the world. Here, we tried everything first, just to be able to say we'd done it.

I pulled myself out of the water and retrieved the three cigarettes I had sneaked from Tío Esteban's stash. We lit up. Chuy and I coughed. Lalo inhaled once or twice and blew the smoke out expertly, like he smoked a pack a day, and then ground the cigarette out on a flat gray rock.

Lalo dipped his head into the water. When he came up for air, he shook his dark, thick hair like a dog, spraying water all over the three of us.

"Me voy," he said matter-of-factly. "I'm going to *la capital*. My aunt knows the director of a good *preparatoria* there. I can get in and live with her."

I wasn't surprised Lalo was finally getting out. He wanted to be a doctor, and he couldn't do that in San Jacinto. He always said he would go. Lalo didn't belong in San Jacinto any more than I did. If he was really leaving, maybe that meant I'd really go, too.

We let the sun dry us for a long time, taking in Lalo's news. "Good," Chuy said finally. "Good. *Y no seas burro*. Don't quit."

He didn't say anything else. We all knew Chuy wasn't going anywhere. All of a sudden, he leaped to his feet. He pulled his wiry frame up the toeholds in the rock at the side of the gorge until he reached the top, then motioned for us to follow.

The three of us sat cross-legged, gazing down at the valley below. The roofs of San Jacinto glinted in the sun. Smoke curled up from the ranchos. Chuy pointed to the East, to two figures in an empty field, one atop a small tractor, the other walking behind.

It was Chuy's father and his older brother, Everardo. They'd vowed not to give up on San Jacinto. Chuy's father had formed a group to try to attract tourists. His mother even had some crazy idea about selling her *indígena* weaving to the *norteamericanos* who came. I didn't know why anyone would want to visit San Jacinto. Chuy knew he was part of his father's big scheme. He seemed resigned to the plan.

"Mira." Chuy pulled his carving out of his pocket. It was one of

his fantastical, mythical animal creations. This one had horns, claws, fangs, and wings, painted in a dozen brilliant colors. Despite its scary looks, the creature seemed good and kind. Like a little boy playing with a toy, Chuy lifted the figure up and made it fly through the air.

I imagined it life-size, carrying me through the sky to the north, across *la línea*, to California.

"I'm going, too," I said suddenly. "I got a letter from Papá. I'm going soon."

Twice before, Papá had announced it was time for me to follow him north. Both times, I'd told Chuy and Lalo that I was going for sure. In the end, there wasn't enough money. Both times, I'd had to admit Papá's failure to make good on his promises.

Chuy and Lalo looked at each other, not at me. Chuy started laughing. Lalo punched my arm playfully. He shook his head in disbelief, scrambled to his feet, and pointed down toward San Jacinto.

"*Ay*, Miguel," Lalo teased. "*No te engañes*. You'll grow old and die here, along with all the other *viejitos*."

I couldn't say anything back to Lalo. Maybe he was right. Papá had let me down before. It could happen again. Half the time, I wasn't even sure if he wanted me with him in California. Wouldn't a father sacrifice whatever it took to bring his only son to his side? If he missed me, really missed me, wouldn't he have come for me himself, a long time ago?

CHAPTER 4

Elena was like the weather vane on top of Señor Mendoza's house. She picked up on every change in the wind, no matter how slight. The day after my birthday, she seemed more alert than ever. She followed me everywhere I went, a silent little shadow. I ignored her. I didn't talk to her, or look her in the eye. I tried to hide it, but she sensed my excitement about Papá's note.

I had to tell Elena about my trip across *la línea*. I couldn't put it off any longer. The sooner she knew the truth, the sooner she could get used to the idea. Late Friday afternoon, I dug out my last few *pesos*. I'd take Elena to San Jacinto. I'd buy her mango ice cream, her favorite, and tell her in public. Maybe she'd behave if we were around other people.

"Let's go to town, Elena," I said. "We'll get some ice cream and hang out."

She squinted her eyes and frowned slightly. I never asked her to have fun with me. She didn't trust my invitation.

"Okay." She was too glad to go to refuse my offer.

On the edge of San Jacinto, Elena stopped. She pulled up her special pink T-shirt, the one Mamá sent from California, so her belly button showed, for the whole world to see.

"You look trashy. Cover up." I reached over with both hands and jerked her T-shirt back down. *"Mensa. Así deshonras nuestro nombre."*

Elena backed up and tugged at her jeans. They moved lower on her hips. She hooked her thumbs in her belt loops, and stuck her chin out defiantly.

"Tú no eres nadie para juzgar," she said. "Who are you to judge?"

I looked her up and down. My sister was pretty. She really didn't need to show skin for boys to notice her. I could scold her about dishonoring the family, but I wasn't her parent, and she knew it. She wasn't about to let me tell her how she could dress.

Elena reached deep into the pocket of her jeans and pulled out an envelope. She'd chewed each fingernail off, way down, a sure sign she was worried about something. Her slender fingers fumbled with the letter.

"Abuelita got this the other day," she confessed. "It's from Mamá. I'm sorry I didn't show it to you before. Don't be mad at me."

I grabbed the paper roughly, jerking it out of Elena's grasp. It was Mamá's usual letter, full of news. There was even a new photo of the twin sisters we'd never seen, three-year-old Maria and Liliana. They sat almost as if they were one, hands clasped. Their lips turned up in identical grins, deep dimples on each cheek. Their noses crinkled up the same way and their faces were framed by curly black hair.

I held the picture by one corner and stared. How was it possible to have sisters I'd never even seen?

"Did you read the last paragraph, Miguel?" Elena asked nervously. "Do you think Mamá means it? Do you think we'll go soon?"

I read it aloud, Elena mouthing each word with me: "We've all been working hard, overtime. We almost have enough money for you, Elena. It won't be long, *te prometo*. Please take good care of Abuelita. You're all she has now."

Elena was ignoring the truth of Mamá's words. I gave her an exasperated look. She knew the way it worked. She knew Papá's plan. Papá went first. Mamá followed. I was next. Elena would be the last. Papá sent for us one by one, waiting until he had money in hand.

"Come on, Elena." I steered her toward the plaza.

Elena got mango, I got chocolate, and we sat side by side on one of the splintered benches at the edge of *la plaza*. Two *señoras*, the ancient Dominguez *cuates*, sat on the far side, string bags at their feet. They folded their arms and gossiped in small voices, their chins on their chests.

El alcalde Don Ramiro sat dozing in a chair, and two men played a slow game of checkers under the tree. Three little boys kicked a soccer ball into and out of the empty wading pool at the edge of the plaza. The blue concrete was cracked and stained with rust from the drain.

"This place is dead," Elena said, licking her cone. She gestured at me, then *la plaza,* and then beyond, to include the whole town.

"Thanks a lot," I said. *"¿Y qué?"*

"You know what I mean." She looked out at the deserted town. There should have been lots of people out, that time of day.

She was right. San Jacinto had been emptied of young men. A few left because they wanted to. Most left because they had to. There was no work, nothing worth doing, just odd jobs here and there that paid a few *pesos,* not enough to feed a family.

"Who'd want to stay anymore?" Elena continued. "Even the girls are leaving now, if they can. Just last month Jesusita left, with that new boyfriend of hers."

"She's sixteen, Elena." I made sixteen sound like sixty—old, really old.

"¿Tú, qué sabes? You're barely fifteen, Miguel. You're hardly even older than me," Elena said angrily.

It was the biggest insult she could think of. It was also how she saw the world. In her mind, the eighteen months that separated us were nothing. If I was old enough to do something, then she was, too.

She stood up and threw the last third of her ice cream cone on the dried-up grass beneath my feet. That was Elena's way of telling me she knew I'd be going. It was her way of telling me what a chicken I was for keeping it a secret.

"It's not fair, Miguel. It's just not fair."

Elena turned and started running down Avenida Principal, out of town. She went right down the center of the road. There weren't any cars to worry about, or boys to impress, so she ran fast, kicking up the red dirt. It mixed with the sweat running down her face, ruining her pretty pink shirt.

CHAPTER 5

By Sunday noon, everyone knew Don Clemente had returned from *la capital*. You couldn't miss his new black Mercedes among the thirty-year-old beat-up, patched-together VW Beetles and Chevy Novas. Most of us didn't have cars at all.

I walked to Don Clemente's compound. It was no longer a house. He'd added two stories, a fancy tiled courtyard, a three-car garage, gates all around, a security system. They said there was even a swimming pool inside. Don Clemente made his money off people like us who needed him.

Juanito stood at Don Clemente's front gate. He slouched against the wrought iron, his hands stuck in his pockets. Juanito was Don Clemente's *bueno para nada* nephew, spoiled by money and too much time on his hands. He screened his uncle's visitors.

I'd hated him ever since we'd both tried out for goalie on the best regional soccer team. It'd been my last shot to make it, and Juanito had beat me out. Everyone believed Don Clemente had bribed the coach. Then Juanito had squandered his chance by drinking and partying, and missing practice. Within two months, he'd been kicked off the team.

Juanito was a jerk, yet I envied him even more than I hated him. Sometimes they felt like the same things, hate and envy. I was jealous of Juanito's easy money. I hated him for his freedom to do what he wanted. The worst thing was that Juanito knew how I felt. I couldn't hide it. He'd take advantage of me if he could.

"Hey, Juanito," I said. "*¿Está tu tío?* I have to see him."

I moved closer. His eyes were red. He covered them quickly with his sunglasses. I smiled to let him know what a loser he was.

"He's busy. You better come back another day," Juanito answered. I was sure this was a lie. It was just Juanito's way of annoying me. I didn't back down.

"Check for me," I replied. "He's expecting me."

I sat down on a carved bench flanked by planters overflowing with bright pink bouganvillea. And then I pulled out a newspaper and read the soccer scores. I wasn't going anywhere until I saw Don Clemente. Juanito sighed, punched a code into the gate, and retreated into the house. I waited an hour.

When Juanito finally returned, he led me wordlessly through the cool courtyard and around the side of the house to the back. Don Clemente sat on a vine-covered patio, his back to me, sipping black coffee. He didn't turn to greet me. He just motioned with his good, right hand to come and sit across from him. With the bad, left hand, he dismissed Juanito.

Don Clemente turned his one good eye to me. He didn't try to hide the dark red burn scars that covered the whole left side of his face. He didn't cover up the empty eye socket. He dared me to stare, to be embarrassed for him. I didn't look away. Don Clemente respected those who weren't afraid to see his ugliness. He leaned down and pulled a packet of papers out of the briefcase at his feet.

"I've heard from Domingo," he announced. "*Tu padre*," he added, as if I might have forgotten Papá's name.

"He's sent money and asked me to make arrangements for you to go." Don Clemente pushed the papers across the table to me.

"Everything you need is there. It's becoming more complicated to make the journey. You must follow the instructions I've provided. Unfortunately, I can no longer vouch for everyone who assists in my operation," he explained. "I've had to rely on some *polleros* whose reputation you should fear."

He stopped to let this sink in. I waited for him to finish.

"But your *coyote*," he continued, pointing to the papers, "the one I've arranged for, he's the best. I've paid him half his fee already. The rest you'll take with you, and pay him when his job is done. He is trustworthy, unlike most."

"Papá trusts you. I'm ready to go."

I said it with confidence, but I felt scared. Don Clemente was not making too much of the risks. Everyone had stories, bad stories. But I couldn't afford to wait. It wasn't getting easier to get across *la línea*; it was getting harder every day.

"Domingo must be desperate to have you with him," Don Clemente continued. "This is the first time he has asked for my help. I would have helped with your mother. I offered to send you, too, a long time ago—and your sister—but Domingo was too proud to accept."

I couldn't believe my ears. What was Don Clemente saying? All Papá had to do was ask and I could've gone, just like that? I'd waited and waited and waited, just because Papá wouldn't ask a rich old man for help? Don Clemente had money coming out of his ears! It especially hurt to know that it was Papá's pride that kept us apart, more than the money. *Orgullo, puro orgullo.*

Don Clemente handed me an envelope with a stack of bills inside. "You know what I owe Domingo. This is a small payment on a large debt."

It was true. Papá had pulled Don Clemente from a roaring fire that burned down his house and killed his wife and daughter. Papá saved him from the flames, but he couldn't save him from becoming bitter.

Money took the place of Don Clemente's family. They said he trafficked in everything. He could get anybody anything he wanted or needed. Anything at all.

But Don Clemente's specialty was why most people ended up knocking on his gate, hat in hand. Everyone in the state knew him as the person who arranged the safest passage north—for the biggest price. If you could scrape together his fees, you went with Don Clemente. They said he'd never lost a single person. *Nunca. Ni una persona.*

We could never afford Don Clemente's price. Whatever money

Papá had sent, Don Clemente was making up the difference himself. I touched the edges of the bills in the envelope. Some of the money came from Papá's cutting lettuce, from Mamá's picking strawberries or weeding and hoeing. The rest of it came from Don Clemente.

"They say you're very quick." He looked at me curiously. "*M'ija* Marisol was like you—smart. Quicker than all the others. She would have gone far."

He paused and rubbed the taut skin around his eye socket. "Read the instructions carefully. Follow them exactly. My people will be expecting you."

"*Gracias,* Don Clemente," I replied. "I'll do as you say."

I stood up and stuck out my hand. Don Clemente grasped it firmly in his. Out of the corner of my eye, I saw Juanito emerge from the shadows at the edge of the patio.

Don Clemente looked at his nephew, then pulled me into a hug. He was stronger than he looked. He held me for a second, then whispered his blessing into my ear, *"Que Dios te acompañe."*

CHAPTER 6

Abuelita poured more *café* into my half-empty cup. The sweet scent of the *canela* that she boiled along with the coffee filled up the kitchen. We sat in friendly silence for many moments, watching the sun rise over the Sierra de los Angeles. We began most mornings that way, ever since Papá and Mamá left years before.

We never talked much. We didn't need to. But the day after I saw Don Clemente, Abuelita had something on her mind. So did I.

"Por fin tu súplica se te ha concedido," Abuelita finally said. "I know how much this means to you."

She reached across the table and entwined my fingers with hers. Dark brown age spots and deep blue veins covered the backs of her hands.

A strand of gray hair fell out of the bun at the back of her head. She tucked it back behind her ear with her free hand, while her other tightened its grip on mine.

"Abuelita," I began. "I have a question for you. Please tell me the truth."

I was sorry as soon as I said it. Abuelita didn't lie. She just gave me a small smile and nodded.

"Is it true what Don Clemente told me, about Papá?" I swallowed hard.

"Sí, m'ijo."

"¿Por qué?, Abuelita? Why? Why?"

"Miguel, your papá must have had his reasons," she answered. "You're going now. That's what counts."

I disengaged my hand from hers, stood up, and turned to the window. "I know. I want to go, but I don't know if I can forgive him."

"You're too hard on people, Miguel. You're hard on Elena," Abuelita answered. "Don't judge your father."

I remained unmoving. I gripped the edge of the windowsill, tightly, until my knuckles turned white. I could not talk back to Abuelita.

"No juzgues, m'ijo," she repeated firmly. It was as close as she ever came to scolding me, and it was the end of the conversation.

"We'll need to slaughter a goat," she said. "I want to have a going-away party for you."

"No, Abuelita," I protested.

Abuelita might need the goat meat later on. Things were tight, really tight. It seemed a waste to use it up. And I didn't want a party. I didn't want any long good-byes. I already had my eyes on *la línea*. I could already feel my feet moving me away.

But Abuelita was determined. So we set the fiesta for three days from then, the night before I was scheduled to leave.

I spent the rest of the day poring over my travel packet. I memorized the routes and the names that Don Clemente had written, each in his flowing, elaborate script. The sheaf of papers, the envelope with the money—all of it seemed too thin, too small to get me where I needed to go, so far north.

But I followed Don Clemente's instructions to the letter. I went to the next town, to the *supermercado* to buy the items I needed: a plastic water bottle, comfortable shoes, and a new backpack with compartments to store everything. I even got a pouch for the money to wear next to my skin, under my shirt. I sneaked everything into the house when Elena was away and hid them in my secret place behind the wall.

And then, for the next three days, I did work for Abuelita that I should have done months before. I hauled, chopped, and stacked a big pile of wood. I repaired several parts of the fence around the corral. I hit my thumb with the hammer twice, and some of the boards hung a little crooked, but at least it was done.

Then I climbed up on the roof to see if I could find the leaks. Even with the little rain we got last winter, Abuelita had to place pots under three places where steady drips of water fell into her kitchen. I patched the leaks, poorly.

"Lo siento, Abuelita," I apologized to her silently as I worked. The truth was, I was no good as a carpenter. The patches on the roof probably wouldn't last.

Finally, I stood and stared at the tomatoes I'd planted two months before. I was an even worse farmer. Bugs had eaten most of them inside out, leaving gaping holes in the flesh. The tomatoes that had escaped the bug attack were small and shriveled. My chiles, next to the tomatoes, had puckered up and fallen off before they ripened.

I picked one of Elena's tomatoes, growing right next to mine. It was round, red, and warm from the sun. I took a big bite. The juice ran down my chin, sweet as sugar. Elena's chiles had grown fat and shiny and long.

"I bet you can't grow ones as good as mine," Elena had taunted in the spring. I took her bet, to shut her up. I checked my plants every day. I tried to do what Elena did with hers. I even gave them extra water, but it was useless. I couldn't compete.

And that wasn't all. When Abuelita put me in charge of the animals last year, the cow quit giving milk and a goat dropped dead for no reason. Under Elena's care, the cow gave more milk than ever. Good thing. We needed the money we'd get from selling it to Señor Gonzalez.

Abuelita said I didn't pay enough attention. She said my mind was always somewhere else. Anybody could grow a plant or raise an animal! But Abuelita didn't scold. She didn't even seem to blame me. To Abuelita, both my strengths and weaknesses were facts, as true as the rising sun or the drought that the sun caused.

"¡Fíjate!" she said last week. I hadn't latched the gate and three chickens disappeared. "Elena is younger, and already she can take care of the *rancho* better than you." There wasn't a bit of rancor in her voice.

Abuelita was right, and I didn't care. Each failure I had on the *rancho* was just more proof to myself that my future lay across *la línea*, in California. If I'd ever belonged in San Jacinto, I didn't belong now.

CHAPTER 7

"Elena, I need your help. *¡Levántate!*" I shook her shoulders roughly. She groaned and pushed my hand away.

"Let me sleep, Miguel. Please, please."

"No, come on. Now!" I pulled off her blankets and jerked the pillow out from under her head. It was already late and I had a lot to do. The goat needed to be slaughtered for the fiesta, and I needed Elena to do it.

An hour later Elena finally made it down to our little barn. I'd already tethered the goat and gathered the tools for the slaughter. Tío used a gunshot to the brain to kill his goats, but Elena preferred a hammer.

"Tío should at least have the guts," she always said, "to get up close to an animal he's going to kill."

Elena held the hammer tightly in her small hands and looked the goat right in the eyes. She took a deep breath and raised the hammer above her head. I turned my eyes, but I heard the sure, solid blow that Elena brought down on the goat's skull. Its knees buckled and it fell to the ground. The goat lay motionless.

"*Pronto,* Miguel," Elena admonished.

I gripped my sharpened knife and cut swiftly through the jugular vein. Together, we strung up the goat and hung it head-downward so the blood would drain out of the body and into the bucket below. The metallic odor of the freshly spilled blood made me gag. I breathed through my mouth to block out the smell, and to stop my stomach from churning.

Elena pulled a wrapped *torta* out of her pocket and gobbled it up in several quick bites. How could she eat with a dead, bloody goat hanging right next to her? She stood, arms crossed. Her eyes moved up and down the carcass.

"We won't get a lot of meat out of this one." She looked at me and waited, daring me to say the truth out loud.

"It should be enough, though, for the fiesta," I replied. "I bet I won't get *cabra* like this in California."

"I was dumb to think Papá would send for both of us," she said. "I know it's your turn."

I picked up the knife and cut a slit from the hind legs to the neck of the goat.

"It won't be long, Elena. Papá and Mamá won't let you stay here alone for long." I continued skinning the goat. I did it the way my godfather taught me, being careful not to contaminate the carcass with feces from the colon.

I felt sick again, this time from the lie I'd just told Elena. We'd both waited years longer than anyone thought. When Papá left, he'd said, "A year, two at the most." It'd been almost seven already. Elena seemed resigned now to staying, as if she'd finally gotten used to the idea. If I told her what Don Clemente had offered, to send us north, she'd just feel worse, right? What good would it do?

"Besides," I said, "I can work when I get to California. There'll be more money if I'm working, too."

"Por favor." Elena rolled her eyes in disgust. "You know Papá will insist you go to school."

I knew the big plan as well as she did. I would be the first *hombre* in the family to graduate from school. Elena would be the first *mujer*. Even after Papá and Mamá left, the plan hadn't changed one bit. We just had to travel through half a continent and learn a whole new language to make it happen. Up to now, Elena and I just accepted that whatever Papá said, we did.

But I'd been nothing but a dumb kid. *¡Menso!* I'd believed everything I'd been told. I held the knowledge about Don Clemente's offer tight inside me. The wasted years of waiting!

I cut off the goat's head at the base of the skull. Elena moved close to me to help with the next part. She took the knife from me and cut open the goat's belly. The stomach and the intestines rolled out, and together we removed the bladder, the liver, and the gall bladder. All of these we threw in the bucket.

We took turns sawing through the bone to get at the heart and lungs. We pulled them out, washed the carcass with cold water, and wiped it dry. We cleaned the tools and rinsed our hands. Finally, Elena picked up the bucket with the discarded organs and walked slowly toward the door. She would take it to the far side of the property and burn it with the rest of the garbage.

At the door, Elena turned. "Don't worry, Miguel. Go ahead. *Vete al norte*. I know what to do. I can take care of myself."

Then she walked slowly across the field. The weight of the offal in the bucket made her list to one side, but she didn't stop until she got to the burn site. She bent and kindled the embers with a handful of dried-up cornstalks.

She threw the organs, one by one, onto the flames. With each throw, she stood straighter and straighter. She watched until the organs had turned to ash and drifted off in the breeze that blew toward the North.

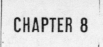

CHAPTER 8

My going-away party was small. There were Tío Esteban and Tía Cristina and my little cousins, José and Daniel. There were our closest neighbors, los Gonzalez, and Doña Maria, my Abuelita's *comadre*.

Elena sat apart from us, with her best friend, Fátima, whispering and telling secrets. Fátima flirted with Chuy, but he paid her no attention. Instead, he served Elena a big plateful of *barbacoa*, then moved to stand right behind her.

We ate goat until we could eat no more. Tío Esteban drank some *Modelos Especiales*, crushing each drained can with his fist. He settled himself on the makeshift bench with his guitar, tuned it, and strummed the chords to "El Rey" and "Cucurucucú Paloma." We got ourselves settled and comfortable around the fire. And then the storytelling began.

"Juanita's husband never returned," Señora Gonzalez announced, as if this were news. She'd told this story about her cousin a hundred times.

"We never heard a word from him. Some say he was lost in the desert. But *I* believe he found a new wife up north."

The part about a new woman had the ring of truth. We all knew Juanita. She was famous for her mean spirit and bad humor. Any one of us would've done anything to escape her.

"Pancho Sanchez told us that his nephew's friend was kidnapped up north, right on the border," said Señor Gonzalez. "They drugged him, and when he woke up, he had a row of stitches in his stomach."

He always began his story in the same way. I leaned forward. What body part would he include this time?

"They took out his kidneys and sold them." Señor Gonzalez grinned, enjoying Tía's gasp of horror.

Tío Esteban laughed and slapped his knee. "Epifanio, you can't live with both kidneys gone. *No es posible*," Tío reminded him.

But Señor Gonzalez didn't care what Tío thought. The more gruesome the story, the better.

"Y a otra mujer," he continued. "They took out her baby and stole it. And then they cut out her female organs and sold them to a barren woman in Saudi Arabia."

He paused, looking around the circle for dramatic effect. "I can't say in this company what they took from the poor woman's husband, but they sold them to an infertile rich old man in Guadalajara who didn't have a son of his own to inherit his millions."

Then we laughed out loud. But my laughter was nervous. The stories seemed different this time, now that I was leaving. Maybe I didn't believe everything Señor Gonzalez said, but the basic idea of kidnapping someone and then selling his organs seemed like it could happen. Weren't there sick people all the time who needed a liver or a heart?

The sun fell down below the horizon. Doña Maria pulled her shawl more tightly around her and inched closer to the fire. Though the evening was still warm, she shivered. We all moved toward the warmth.

Doña Maria put her fingers lightly on my forearm. *"M'ijo,"* she murmured, "When you travel through the wasteland of the desert, you must take special care."

No one ever gave away the secrets of Don Clemente's operation. But Doña Maria believed, like all of us, that I'd walk through the desert to cross *la línea*.

"In that place of desolation," she continued, "a ghost now walks at night. They say it is *La Llorona*. That I can't say for sure. But this much I know. She'll attempt to lure you away from your path. Cover your ears so you don't hear her wailing. Don't make the mistake many have made, of following her."

She looked me in the eye, her voice quiet. "Those who pursue her are never found again. Their bodies dry up and fly away with the wind."

I reminded myself that I didn't believe in *La Llorona*. It was just a story that everybody told. There were a hundred different versions; of course one of them would put the wailing woman in the desert. But who knew what might happen crossing *la línea*? Lots of people were never heard from again.

"How do you like my *chupacabra*?" Chuy asked suddenly, changing the subject. Out of his pocket came his latest carving.

Chuy's "goatsucker" figure had sharp spines all the way up and down its back and claws sticking out from its hands and feet. Chuy had painted it bright green. Its glowing red eyes reflected the light from the dying fire. The thing looked real, and evil.

"The *chupacabras* have migrated north," Tío Esteban said with authority. "They're no longer satisfied with draining the blood from cattle and other farm animals."

Reports of mutilated goat and cow carcasses, their blood sucked dry by the *chupacabra* monster, came from all over Mexico. We'd all heard this part about the creatures' move into new territory. And the last time he told it, Tío even claimed that the *chupacabras* were really aliens, here to colonize Earth.

"They now prey on humans, especially those out alone, at night, with no protection," he cautioned.

He didn't look in my direction, but everyone knew the story was pointed at me. Maybe the *chupacabras* were imaginary, but other creatures out in the desert were real. A scorpion was real. A *culebra* was real. People died all the time from their poison.

Tío took Chuy's carving in his hand, turning it around and upside down. He studied the eyes, the tongue, the nose. Then he looked directly at the *chupacabra*'s rear end.

"Actually," he said, "this part looks a lot like *el presidente*, don't you think?"

Then everyone laughed and joked and told more *La Llorona* and *chupacabra* stories, each one wilder than the one before it. They told these tales with a purpose, to comfort each other, and to comfort me. The crazier the stories got, the less we needed to believe them.

But mostly, they told these stories to avoid telling the ones that were one hundred percent true, the ones that we *had* to believe.

Fátima didn't tell how her brother Eleuterio left suddenly one day, only to be found two weeks later, suffocated to death, stuffed into an abandoned tractor trailer one mile north of *la línea*, dead with twenty-six others.

Lalo didn't tell how his father was robbed, beaten, and left for dead in the desert. He didn't tell how he came back, deaf in one ear, the fingers of his right hand gone. He didn't tell how his father now spent his days in a darkened room, speaking to no one.

And no one spoke of the Martinez sisters, ten-year-old Juana and twelve-year-old Julietta, sent for by their parents, sent across the desert with a *coyote*, and never heard from again. No one speculated on the fate of the girls. No one wanted to say how they might have died or, even worse, how they might still live.

And for many, many minutes, no one spoke at all. Finally, one by one, they wished me well. They hugged me and shook my hand, pressing a few *pesos* into my palm. They left, walking away into the darkness.

CHAPTER 9

Lalo, Chuy, and I sat in a tight circle around the *barbacoa* pit, watching the fire die down to red embers and white ash. We poked at the coals with sticks, and bright yellow sparks flew out into the night.

Elena moved behind us, cleaning up from the party. She worked quickly, but silently. She carted dishes and food to the house, gave a bone to the dog, and took scraps to the animals in the barn.

Finally, she threw the rest of the garbage on the coals, right in front of me, a messy glop of paper and grease. The fire popped and sputtered angrily. It leaped to life. A long tongue of flame rose up next to my foot. I moved back quickly. I turned to give Elena a piece of my mind, but she was gone. The door to the house slammed shut.

"What's up with her?" Chuy asked. *"¿Qué tiene?"*

He motioned toward Elena's pile of burning garbage, now a big black blob. It bubbled and writhed.

I shrugged. "Nothing. She's just mad because I'm going. She'll get over it."

Chuy kicked at a log, sending more sparks into the air. "If you say so, Miguel."

He turned and looked at our *casita,* and the light that lit the room Elena and I shared. Her shadow moved back and forth. Then the room went dark. Chuy turned back and stared into the flames, silent.

Suddenly, Lalo unbuttoned his shirt. Under it, he was wearing an America soccer jersey I'd never seen, just like the kind I'd always wanted. He quickly stripped off the shirt and carefully folded it into quarters.

"I got this from my cousin." He placed the jersey in my hands. "I thought you'd like it. *No es nueva*. It's secondhand. Don't get too excited." But he looked at me sideways, checking my reaction.

"It's perfect," I replied. I pulled it over my head, fingering the silky fabric.

Chuy reached deep into his front right pocket. With one swift movement, he pulled out his carving knife, placed it in the palm of my hand, and closed my fist tightly around it. I felt the smooth bone handle, still warm from Chuy's touch, and the switch that released the razor-sharp blade.

"You might need this," he said.

I knew this was his only knife. It was the only knife he'd ever carved with. Neither of us spoke. The stories from earlier, told and untold, hung in the night air.

I was embarrassed. Lalo and Chuy had not only given me their most precious possessions; they'd given me the *only* things of value they owned.

And I felt ashamed. I had nothing for either of them. Worse than that, I hadn't even thought about giving them a present. I stood, shifted my body, and stuck my hands in my pockets. I kicked the ground with the toe of one shoe, and looked out into the night.

But Lalo and Chuy didn't care. They didn't expect a thing from me. They knew me and my life upside down and inside out. How could I give what I didn't have?

Lalo let me off the hook. A familiar sparkle appeared in his eye. "I have an idea. Let's meet in ten years, when we're twenty-five. What do you say, Miguel?"

He said it as a challenge. He said it in the same way he used to dare us to smoke or drink or skip school. It seemed like a present I could give. It was a promise I could keep.

Chuy jumped on the idea. "Yeah! *Diez años. Aquí mismo, en* San Jacinto. Okay, Miguel? Okay?"

I nodded. We shook hands, sealing the promise we'd made. Our eyes traveled from one to the other. These were my best friends. I could see in their eyes the belief that somehow we'd always be the same, that we'd always feel the same.

Papá had been gone seven years. It seemed like forever. Ten years was an eternity. Chuy and Lalo couldn't know something I'd learned from Papá's absence: that it wouldn't be long before I forgot the way Chuy tilted his head when he listened, the way Lalo crossed his arms when he talked, how much Chuy loved to joke, or how much Lalo hated to lose.

My friends still believed they would somehow remember everything about me. I knew they would forget.

CHAPTER 10

I slept badly and, for once, it wasn't Elena's fault. Every time I started to fall asleep, I jerked awake. When I finally got up before dawn, Elena's bed was rumpled but empty. I guessed where she was. I knew she didn't want to watch me leave in person.

I surveyed everything I'd packed for the journey and pulled Don Clemente's packet from its hiding place. I put the money in my pouch, checking to be sure it didn't bulge beneath my clothing. I packed Lalo's soccer jersey and stuck Chuy's knife into my front right pocket.

I looked in the cracked mirror above the dresser one last time. I saw the same high cheekbones, the same familial dimples, the same slightly hooked nose.

But I hardly recognized me. Somehow, it seemed my outside hadn't caught up with my inside. There were my very same deep-set almost-black eyes and eyebrows that swooped up at the ends. How could I look the same and feel so different? I peered again at my reflection—the same old face, the same old Miguel.

I picked my way in the half-light of the dawning morning down to the corral and the little barn. Sure enough, there in the darkness, I could just make out Elena's form. She was curled up on the straw, lying next to the dog and the cow. This was her other bed. The gentle breathing of the animals, the warmth, and the sweet smell of the hay had always been able to put her to sleep.

I left Elena alone. I wasn't going to tell her I was sorry I was leaving and she was staying. Why should I? She hadn't wished me good luck. She hadn't even said she'd miss me. She'd said nothing to me, nothing at all. Well, she'd have to get over it, sooner or later.

Abuelita had prepared some food for the first part of my trip. She packed and unpacked it several times, fussing over where it fit best. She finally tucked the oranges and apples away on the sides of my backpack and lay the tacos on top.

"I have something else for you, *m'ijo*." Abuelita lifted her *Virgen de Guadalupe* medallion from around her neck.

I'd never seen her take it off, not once in my whole life. The bright blue of the Virgin's mantle reflected the light of the sun as its first rays peeked through the window.

A piece of the silver chain caught in her hair. I untangled it, but a few strands of gray remained in the links. I left them. Abuelita gathered up the chain and the medallion, pressed it into my hand, and placed her hand on my head.

"*M'ijo, que La Virgen te guarde, te proteja y te cuide con todo su amor en tus caminos,*" she began. Her low, raspy voice was strong, but her hand trembled.

"*Y que La Virgen te abra los ojos hacia todos los que tienen menos que tú.*" This was an old blessing, but the words felt new. This time, the blessing was for me.

Except for Elena, who cried at anything, we were a dry-eyed family. No one cried at leaving, no matter how long we'd be separated. We liked to pretend we'd be gone just a few days, instead of years. We liked to fool ourselves that the absence was easier to take that way.

I looked up at Abuelita. This time, the tears rolled freely down both of our faces.

She'd been my mother. I'd been her son. There was no sense pretending we'd see each other again. She was old. I wouldn't return for many years. I might not return at all.

CHAPTER 11

It took me three hours to walk to the city, but it felt like minutes. I wanted to catch the next bus north, at noon. Then I'd be slightly ahead of the timetable set out by Don Clemente. I wandered around, peering into shop windows and pushing my way through the crowded stalls in the *mercado*.

The city was a crossroads for a steady stream of people headed north, south, east, and west. Cars and trucks belched black exhaust that burned my eyes. The taxi drivers blasted their horns and a loud *whomp-whomp* of music blared from the speakers of other cars.

Midmorning, I stood in the shade cast by the giant wall of the cathedral and pulled the last of the *tacos de cabrito* out of my bag. The tortillas had turned hard and cold, but I ate every bite.

Two hours early, I found my way to the bus station. What if the seats were sold out? I didn't think I could stand to wait for the next bus. I wasn't the only worried one. Dozens of anxious travelers sat side by side, their belongings stacked at their feet. I bought my ticket, found a seat on a worn wooden bench, and settled down to wait.

An older couple sat across from me. They propped their legs up on a huge, bulging suitcase. He wore an old black suit, the shoulders dusted by dirt. She, too, wore black, a long dress with shiny buttons. In her hands she held a small photograph, its edges tattered and worn. She caressed the face on the photo with her index finger. I decided they must be going to the funeral of their only son.

A young father and mother, near my age, sat on top of two boxes tied together with rope. They passed a baby back and forth, but it cried nonstop anyway. Two more string bags held some fruit and drinks, a bean pot, a *molcajete*, a box of soap. This was everything they owned in the world. I thought they must be headed to *la capital* to try out a different life. They'd still be poor there. It would just be a different kind of poor.

I felt quick and light and alert. Everyone else seemed burdened, loaded down. My backpack and my pouch weighed no more than a feather.

The bus finally pulled up to the station. The mother and father with the baby stowed their boxes, mounted the stairs, and sat at the front. An *india*, wearing a bright, multicolored skirt and blouse, slid into the second seat. A shawl covered most of her face, for modesty. She grabbed the ends and pulled it tighter around her neck. She carried only a small string bag. I decided she was going to help her sister who had just had a baby.

I made my way to the back of the bus and claimed a seat next to a window. Three young men settled down behind me. They didn't wear their traditional pants and shirts, but I could tell they, too, were *indios*. Triquis, maybe, Zapotecos or Mixtecos. They sat shoulder to shoulder, speaking softly in their own language. Maybe they didn't speak Spanish. Probably they just didn't want me to understand.

Two more young men grabbed the seat in front of me. One wore a New York Yankees cap facing backward on his head. His T-shirt had a faded cartoon drawing of a square-faced kid with spiky yellow hair. The other man wore an Oakland Raiders cap pointed forward and a ragged sweatshirt with a Notre Dame logo.

"What's the name of the guy they told us about? Do you think we can find him? What if we can't find him?" one asked anxiously.

"Would you stop asking me that?" the other replied. "I already told you ten times." He used the annoyed tone of an older brother, one I used with Elena when I wanted her to shut up. I guessed by their accents they came from Guatemala, or maybe Honduras.

A black man slid into the seat across the aisle. He was traveling alone and light, like me. I nodded at him slightly. He returned the nod with one of his own, adding a shy smile.

He carried one small backpack held together in some places by duct tape and in others by crude hand stitching. Out of this he pulled a portable CD player. He fiddled with the earphones, adjusted the volume, and settled back, listening intently. Who was he? Where was he from? I finally decided he was a tourist, probably not as poor as he looked.

Several other men entered the bus. Each was single. Most traveled alone. I counted a total of fifteen young men, including myself. I bet all of us had the same destination, somewhere across *la línea*. Here we were together, close enough to touch.

There, up north, one might go to Chicago, another to Atlanta, or Michigan. What were the other places I'd heard about? Oregon? Yakima? Oklahoma? Someplace called Little Rock? Some were cities, it seemed. Maybe others were states. I wasn't sure. There was California, of course. I knew all about California.

Finally, yet another man sat right next to me. I let out a big sigh. I wanted to be alone so I could stretch out a little and sleep. I knew I needed to rest when I could. But he was barely seated before he started talking, a fast-flowing river of words, as if he'd been starved for conversation.

"*Hola. Me llamo* Javier. You can call me Javi," he began. "What's your name? I'm from El Salvador. You're from here, right?"

He paused only long enough to kick his backpack beneath the seat in front of him. He had silver hair and deep wrinkles around his mouth and the corners of his eyes. I looked closer. He was a lot older than anyone else on the bus.

"This is a good bus. I can tell already. You can always tell by the driver," he continued without taking a breath. "I've been on two that broke down. Where are you going? Maybe we could go together. It's boring to travel alone."

He looked at me hopefully. Don Clemente had warned me not to give away my route or my contacts. Besides, I didn't want the burden of another human being.

So I lied. "I'm going to *la capital* to stay with my brother and sister-in-law."

Javier's shoulders slumped in disappointment. But within minutes, his friendly talk started up again. Over the next hour, I found out he came from the mountains of El Salvador somewhere. He used to work on a big coffee plantation. He left behind his wife and two children.

"I had no choice," he explained. "The coffee prices went in the toilet. With no work, no money, what was I supposed to do?

"I'm going north, to New York, where my brother works in a restaurant. He can get me a job. Within a short amount of time, I'll have money to send for the family."

He paused momentarily and looked at me more closely. "You must be about the same age as my boy, Eduardo. He wanted to come with me, but of course he had to stay to help out the family. He wasn't happy about it.

"You're not going to *la capital*, are you?" Javi said suddenly. It wasn't really a question. He hadn't believed my story. I've always been a bad liar.

"You could come with me, you know," he offered.

He waited for me to answer. "This is my second try. I've learned a few things, and sometimes it's good to have someone to watch your back."

I said a silent thanks to Don Clemente. With his people and his *coyote,* I didn't need anyone else. If Javier had already tried once, and failed, I'd be better off by myself, alone. The last thing I wanted was an old man tagging along with me. How much help could someone like that be, anyway?

"Gracias," I murmured. "I've got my own plans."

CHAPTER 12

I leaned my head against the dirt-streaked window and closed my eyes. What was Javi saying now? I'd quit paying attention. Words just bubbled out of his mouth. He didn't seem to notice that I wasn't really listening.

I felt the bus stop. I opened my eyes, straining to see through the grime. Three federal police cruisers blocked the road in front of us, and a white transport bus stood empty by the side of the road.

Javier sat up straight beside me. "This is bad news," he said. "The *federales* have a special internal procedure to look for people like me. You know, people traveling through Mexico to get to the North."

"You're lucky," he continued. "The *federales* won't bother you. After all, you're Mexican, a citizen. *Es tu país.* You belong here."

I was relieved. I had my school identification, which should work for this check. But I was now suddenly worried for Javier. "Pretend you're Mexican," I said. "How will they know?"

He laughed. "The first time I tried to come north, they tricked me with one of their questions, the ones they use to separate people like me from Mexican citizens. They asked me how many stars the Mexican flag has. I guessed and said three. They laughed at me and sent me right back across the border to Guatemala."

Javier sighed loudly, then continued, "But there's no end to the tricks, is there? Besides, just listen to me. If they ask me to talk, they'll know."

It was true. His accent wasn't like mine, and not like any of the accents I'd heard before in Mexico.

A fat *federal* boarded the bus slowly. His bulky figure blocked the front window. From under his cap, I saw his eyes move from passenger to passenger. He lifted up the driver's microphone, his breathing still heavy from the short climb up the bus steps.

"Exit with your belongings. Line up by the side of the bus in single file," he commanded.

His eyes continued to glide over us, checking to see who might resist. Everyone did exactly as he said. No one even complained. He smirked. To him, we were just a bunch of *pobres,* now under his control. *¡Buey!*

Outside the bus, I found myself near the end of the line. The *federal* strutted back and forth in front of the passengers. His name tag glinted in the sun. "Capitán Morales" it read. His gut hung out over his belt. He clutched his clipboard importantly, tapping it rhythmically with his pen.

"This is a routine check," he announced. "I'll ask each of you a few questions, and then you'll be free to reboard the bus with your things."

At the front of the line was the young couple with their baby. Morales asked them many questions, too many for a routine check. The father answered each quickly. Still, the *capitán* continued to ask, and ask again.

I saw the father reach into his pocket. He turned his back to us and I knew he was taking out money to pay off the *federal.* He didn't want trouble for his family. He just wanted to get where he was going.

The *capitán* was making an example of the father. The message was loud and clear: "Look how easy this can be, you poor fools. I can mess up your day, so don't make it hard on yourself." Morales had practice getting money out of poor people.

My stomach turned over. How much could I offer? What would Morales accept? What would he do if I said I had nothing? I needed every single *peso.* I couldn't give him the bribe he was after. What good would it do to have only part of the money for my *coyote*?

The *capitán* moved down the line slowly. He pulled the two brothers with sports caps apart from the others. They had no papers. They had suspicious accents. Mostly, they had no money for bribes. *La mordida* was not an option. Morales would send them south to Guatemala, along with the other young men who couldn't pull enough money out of their pockets.

Included in this group was the black man I couldn't figure out. He gave me a small, sad smile. He didn't seem surprised to be singled out in this way. Maybe this had happened to him many times before.

Finally, the *capitán* stopped directly in front of the small *indígena*. Ever so slowly, he pulled the shawl down from her head, revealing her face. I'd know that profile even at a thousand meters.

"Elena!" I gasped.

She turned, looked at me, and whispered, "Miguel." The color drained from her face and her lower lip began to tremble. She took one tentative step toward me, but the *capitán* grabbed her arm and pushed her back roughly. Elena tripped on her shawl, falling to her knees.

Capitán Morales turned toward me. I could almost see his brain working, very slowly. Who was Elena? Who was I? How were we connected? All he could figure out was that Elena wasn't who she pretended to be. Anyone in Mexico would know that her face didn't match the *india* clothing she wore.

And then, at that very moment, the Yankee-capped young man, one of the brothers, muttered, *"Cobarde."*

He said it just loud enough for the *capitán* to hear. A guy like Morales must've heard bad words many times in his career. He must've been called lots of names. But to be called a coward, that was the worst. So much for his *machismo*!

I saw the *capitán*'s eyes change. The *capitán* felt disrespected, and he'd been disrespected enough already for one day. I knew that he'd stop trying to figure out who belonged in Mexico and who didn't. He didn't care who we were, where we came from, or where we were going. Morales would make us pay for his bad day.

For the first time, I was afraid.

Within minutes, Capitán Morales and two other armed *fed-*

erales escorted us onto the transport bus, all fifteen men I'd counted, plus Elena. No one protested. What would be the point? I sat, once again, next to Javier. I couldn't imagine how he felt, having to go back for a second time. Javi muttered quietly, repetitive and rhythmic phrases I couldn't make out. Prayers, probably.

Elena was in back of me. I felt her eyes bore into the back of my head, but I refused to turn and look at her.

The bus chugged slowly, to the south, toward the border with Guatemala. I remained motionless for many hours, watching the sun set on the wrong side of the bus. Morales would dump us on the other side of the river. My plan—Don Clemente's carefully laid plan—was in ruins. And Elena was to blame.

CHAPTER 13

The bus stopped just once before the border, in the pitch-black of night. One by one, the *federales* left the bus, walked away into the darkness, and quickly returned. I guessed they were going to pee. Elena had never been able to wait to go, and I knew she was suffering with every bump in the road. Well, fine. She deserved to suffer a little.

As for me, my butt hurt, my neck ached, and my legs were cramped from being doubled up. Morales had forbidden us to stand or change seats. The complaining finally began.

"*Ay*, Capitán, let us out, just for a minute," one called out. "What do you want, a big mess on the bus?"

"*Usa una botella,*" Morales sneered. He motioned for the driver to get going, sat back down, and pulled his cap over his eyes. Several men cursed him quietly.

"They're no better than the worms that feed on a dead corpse," Javi said sourly, nodding his head in the direction of our jailers.

He rubbed his forehead with both hands and then ran his hands through his hair, attempting to comb it with his fingers. He shrugged, raising his hands palms up.

"But their work will be for nothing. We'll all come back, all of us." Javier looked around the bus to confirm his opinion.

"This isn't the first time for them, either." He pointed at the two brothers. Then he paused. "For them, it's a minor setback, nothing more."

He motioned to the black man across the aisle. "And that guy? He's come all the way from Brazil! Do you know how far that is? He'd never let an idiot like Morales get in his way."

Javier studied me curiously for a moment. Then he turned slightly in his seat to catch a glimpse of Elena behind us. "*¿Quién es?*

Your girlfriend? What are you going to do about her? She's a liability, you know. She'll slow you down."

Elena leaned forward, placing her chin on the edge of our seat. Her head was right between ours. "I won't slow anybody down because I'm traveling alone. And I'm *not* his girlfriend, I'm his sister. I already told him I know what to do and he doesn't need to worry about me."

Elena spoke to Javier. She said it as if I weren't even there.

"Actually," I said to Javi, ignoring Elena, "she's only thirteen years old. You can tell what a baby she is by how she behaves. Now I'll be forced to change all my plans and take her back home. She's so selfish, she didn't think that far ahead."

"It's her fault we ended up like this," I continued. "Most of us would be all the way to the border by now, if it weren't for her."

I only half believed this, but I said it anyway to hurt Elena. It felt good to say the things I'd been thinking all night long.

Javi was grinning. He didn't seem to care who won the argument. He was just enjoying the entertainment.

"That's not true. That ugly, fat *capitán* would've let me back on the bus if Miguel hadn't called out my name the way he did." Elena's voice got louder with each word. By then, half the bus was listening.

"And just who does he think is really selfish? *He's* the one that was going to leave me all by myself in San Jacinto. I know how to get north, and I'm going to do it."

Elena stood up, gripping the metal edge of the seat with both hands. "I'm not going back to San Jacinto, not ever!" she screamed over my head.

Capitán Morales stood up at the front of the bus. He stared long and hard at Elena, hitched up his pants, and yelled, "Shut up, all of you!" Morales turned back toward the driver. *"¡Cállensen!"*

Just then, the bus lurched. Morales lost his balance. He reached for the seat nearest him, missed the back, and fell on his knees in the aisle. He grunted and pushed himself up. His pants fell down. We all could see most of his giant naked butt.

Elena giggled quietly behind me. Javier's laugh began low in his gut, and ended in a series of loud snorts that flew out his nose, like a donkey's bray. It ended in a giant wheeze. I began to laugh. I couldn't help it. Then everyone started to laugh, with Javi, and at Morales. For the moment, we didn't care if Morales got back at us.

But Morales made like it never happened. At the front of the bus, in front of us all, he adjusted his uniform jacket and sweat-stained cap. He pulled up his pants once more, trying to get them over his bulging gut.

Finally, he withdrew his pistol from its holster and inspected it casually. The barrel gleamed in the half light of the dawning sun glowing through the window of the bus. It was all an act, like his earlier shakedown, but it worked. Silence fell over the bus again.

Javier's wheezing that had begun with his laughter hadn't stopped. His chest rose and fell with his efforts to take in air, but he didn't stop smiling.

He leaned over and whispered in my ear, "I wonder if this guy is as stupid as he looks. I think he might be. I'm going to find out."

With that, Javier scrunched down, settled his head against the metal edge on the back of the seat, and closed his eyes. I fell asleep to the sound of Javi's breaths, loud and insistent.

CHAPTER 14

My stomach growled loudly, waking me from my nap. I kicked my backpack angrily. I regretted gobbling down every bite of Abuelita's tacos and fruit the day before. Suddenly, without a word said, food appeared. It came out of pockets, duffel bags, backpacks, paper sacks. Someone peeled oranges and passed the pieces around. My share was two small slices. The black man took out a *torta*, unwrapped it, and tore it into rough chunks to share.

There were pieces of taco, tortilla, a few *chicharrones*, some dry cookies. Elena dug up a brown, squishy banana. She broke off an end piece and passed it up to me. She knew it was the only part of a banana I liked. She meant it as a small peace offering. I ate it, but I didn't feel like making peace with her. I wouldn't ever forgive her stupidity.

Out the window, I saw the landscape had changed. A thick forest, almost a jungle, lined the rutted road. The bus slowed to a crawl. A long line of people walked single file on both sides of the road, most headed the opposite direction from us. Through the front window of the bus, I could barely see the outline of a town in the distance.

A lazy green river snaked along the road part of the way. Discarded plastic bottles, car tires, and rusty cans littered the banks. A small flotilla of makeshift rafts ferried dozens of people across the slow-moving water from Guatemala to Mexico.

Javi pointed. "Look," he said knowingly. "See how easy it is here? I told you. You pay a few *pesos*, they bring you back across."

Small open-air stands with palm-frond roofs sold a variety of goods: food, cigarettes, beer, clothing of all kinds, hats. Several stalls advertised notaries who could provide "expert assistance with documents." I laughed to myself. This was the border. You could buy anything here. You could get anything here. You just had to pay for it.

Javier nudged me with his elbow. "There, up there, that's the bridge we cross. Over there is Guatemala."

He pointed, then shifted his body closer. "But why should we have to cross over, just to come back the same day, or the next? Doesn't that seem ridiculous to you?

"We'll stop before the bridge for procedures. You know, the usual paperwork. They'll take us out of the bus to escort us across."

He leaned his head even closer, and whispered in my ear. "Watch me carefully. I'm going to try an old trick that's proved useful several times in the past. If you see a chance, escape."

Javier looked around the bus at all the young men. He turned in his seat and looked at Elena, then at me again. He smiled to himself, as if he had a private joke.

"Pass the word to everyone," he said. "Tell them what I told you. Be quiet about it."

I whispered Javi's instructions to Elena and to the brothers in front of us. I told them to pass it on. I leaned across the aisle and delivered them to the black man. His brows knit together as I spoke. He leaned forward to relay the message.

Before long, the news of a possible escape traveled the length of the bus. We sat higher in our seats. For the first time since the disaster with Morales began, I felt hopeful. Even if Javi's scheme failed, whatever it was, we would have tried.

As Javier predicted, the bus ground to a halt next to a small adobe building. A slight, mousy man in a uniform motioned to the *federales*. One exited the bus and huddled with the border official. Straight ahead was the bridge, a rickety structure that looked like it couldn't support the weight of a bicycle, much less a bus.

Morales ordered us off and herded us close to the building. I clutched my backpack and eyed Javi sideways, waiting and wondering. Morales gave us a mean look, fondled his pistol in its holster, and moved out of earshot. He continued to stab at his clipboard with his index finger, trying to make some point. The immigration official appeared to disagree, shaking his head.

The other *federales* wandered over toward Morales. Papers were passed back and forth, heads bent over Morales's clipboard, check marks were made. I was sure some money would change hands. They'd pay each other to keep quiet about all the things each was doing wrong.

Morales's face got redder by the moment. I could imagine him running drugs or guns or prostitutes. We were probably nothing to him, just a little extra pocket change.

Javi whispered in my ear, "He wants to dump us like trash in Guatemala. Well, he's got a surprise coming. Watch me ruin Morales's day."

Javi began to walk toward the officials. He swayed and stumbled, clutching his throat and choking. Then he fell flat on the ground, right in front of Morales. His eyes rolled back in his head until I could see only the whites. His legs, then his arms began to jerk violently. White foam appeared at the corners of his mouth. He wailed, a sound more animal than human.

Javi had said it was an old trick, but it looked like the real thing. A crowd gathered, mixing with our group. Morales looked at Javi like he was some strange creature he'd never seen before.

Finally, Morales began a feeble attempt to control Javi's flailing limbs. He got his beefy arms around Javi's chest and yelled to the other officials, "Get over here! Get this guy out of here!"

I grabbed Elena's hand and took one slow step back. I made eye contact with the two brothers, and the black man. We nodded to each other. Already, the *indios* and five or six of the other men had disappeared. They'd left quickly and silently, melting into the crowd that surrounded Javier. It was as if they had never existed.

I turned and ran, dragging Elena after me. I heard screams, gunshots, and Morales's booming voice. "*¡Alto! ¡Alto!* Halt or I'll shoot!"

More shots rang out. Was Morales mad enough to shoot Javi right there? Had he figured out it was a trick? Javi had taken a big risk. He had more to lose than we did, a lot more. After all, he had a family to think about, a son my age, a daughter, a wife. And he was a lot older, ancient, older even than Papá. He'd already tried once to make it, and had failed.

If he escaped Morales, if he made it across from Guatemala again, he'd be desperate. Who wouldn't?

We ran faster than we'd ever run before. I held Elena's hand tighter than I needed to. I wouldn't lose her. I intended to put her on the first bus that I could find home, to San Jacinto. And then I'd go north, alone.

I didn't even want to think about what Morales would do if he caught us.

CHAPTER 15

We had two choices for escape: back in the direction the bus traveled, cutting into the dense forest around the bend, or straight toward the center of town. I chose the second. We ran headlong into the crowds of people in the *zócalo* and the *mercado* next to it. Maybe we could blend in and lose Morales forever.

"Miguel," Elena huffed. "Stop for a minute."

She jerked her hand away and trotted around the back of a little stand selling piles of knock-off watches, cheap jewelry, sodas, snacks, sports caps, and newspapers. She leaned against the back of the stall. I tried to catch my breath, but the air was so humid it felt like I was breathing in water. Sweat streamed down our faces, necks, and arms and dripped to the ground.

"I can't run anymore in this." Elena put down her string bag and motioned to her clothing.

Her long *indígena* skirt grazed her feet, the hem now torn and dirty. Her toes peeked out from a pair of sandals. Her shawl had fallen off one shoulder and one end dragged on the ground.

I looked around. We had ended up behind a long line of stalls on one edge of the *mercado*. Except for a few stacks of boxes, the narrow, shaded passageway was empty. It wasn't a bad place to hide for a while. We could at least catch our breath.

Elena squatted down and opened her bag. "Turn around, Miguel. I'm going to change."

She pulled out a pair of jeans, her sneakers, and a T-shirt. I ignored her command, took her bag, and opened it further. There was only one other shirt and a sweater. At the bottom was the little purse of Mamá's letters and Elena's wallet. I grabbed it quickly, holding it over my head, beyond her reach.

"Give it back, Miguel. That's my money." She reached for the wallet. I swatted her hand away.

I sat down on the dirt cross-legged, opened the wallet, and took out the money. I counted the bills one by one, very slowly, looking pointedly at Elena in between each. It was not as much as Don Clemente gave me. It wasn't enough to pay for a *coyote,* I knew that. Still, it was a lot of money for a thirteen-year-old to be carrying around.

"Where did you get this? *¿Dónde? ¿Dónde?*" I demanded. I couldn't imagine how she got her hands on so much cash. It couldn't have come from Abuelita or anyone else in the family.

Elena stared at the ground sullenly. "It's enough to go north, isn't it? That's all that matters." She started to cry, just like she always did when she got into trouble.

"*¡Chillona!*" I hissed at her. "You got us into this mess. I'd be all the way to the border by now, if it weren't for you."

I grabbed her wrist tightly and twisted. "You will tell me where you got this money. Now."

"Ouch, Miguel. Let go. You're hurting me," Elena complained. Her eyes again filled with tears. I tightened my hold. I didn't care if I hurt her. I hoped I hurt her.

Elena was silent for several minutes. Then she gave in.

"Juanito," she murmured, continuing to look at the ground.

"What? *¿Qué dijiste?*" I couldn't believe I'd heard her correctly.

"Juanito," she repeated. "He gave me the money. I went to him and asked and he just gave it to me."

She took up a handful of dirt and let it fall slowly through her fingers to the ground. She did this over and over, as if she was sifting the earth for something she lost and couldn't find.

"How could you, Elena? *Juanito es un vendido.* He's a sell-out—he would sell out his own people." I was disgusted. "We'll never be able to pay him back. Never. He'll always want more."

I'd never told Elena how much I hated Juanito for using Don

Clemente to get on the soccer team. But she lived in San Jacinto just like I did, and in San Jacinto, everyone knew what everyone else was like. Juanito wasn't just a lazy cheater who cut corners to get what he wanted. He was dangerous. If he wasn't already, he'd soon be trafficking drugs for one of the big cartels. And he wouldn't let Don Clemente get in his way.

"Why, Elena? And how? How did you do all of this?" I said coldly.

In a small monotone, Elena told me how she watched every move I made in the weeks before I left. She explained how she looked in my secret hiding place behind the wall to find Don Clemente's instructions. She told me how she searched out Juanito at the *cantina* where he hung out, how she went right up to him and asked for the money, how he just pulled it out of his pocket as if it were spare change.

"How could you make everyone worry? What about Abuelita? How could you leave her alone? You were supposed to stay and take care of her!" I said angrily. *"¿No tienes vergüenza?*

"And didn't you realize it wasn't enough money to follow Don Clemente's plan? Didn't you understand what would happen?"

Elena wiped the tears off her face, snuffled, and blew her nose into the hem of her skirt.

"You don't care about me, Miguel. You only care about you, and your plans. You never cared about leaving me alone. I'm the one who wanted to go north more than anyone. But you never bothered to ask how I felt, and you wouldn't understand anyway," Elena said finally.

"We're going home, Elena. We're going home together. We'll take the money back to Juanito, every single *peso*. And then . . . I don't know. . . ." I paused. I felt defeated.

I'd have to talk to Don Clemente again. I'd need to start all over. And I'd have to call Papá and have him threaten Elena with her life if she moved even one foot out of San Jacinto.

In the end, Elena did what I said. We changed clothes and I

bought us caps and cheap sunglasses. Elena pushed her hair up under her cap and I pulled mine down over my eyes. We didn't want Morales to recognize us easily. He might still be in town.

I took the money Juanito had given Elena and tucked it into my own pouch for safekeeping. I left Elena at a small restaurant where we splurged on *huevos con chorizo*. I went to the bus station to check the schedule. The next bus to San Jacinto left at six o'clock the following morning. I bought two one-way tickets home.

In the evening, I took Elena into the only movie theater in town. We sat through a double feature to kill time. The screen was wavy and torn and the sound system crackled, the words out of synch with the picture. The air conditioner worked off and on, from hot to cold to hot again.

I sat and watched and remembered nothing of the movie. I didn't think about anything at all. I didn't want to plan or hope or dream again, not ever again.

Then, late at night, I searched for a place for us to sleep. The hotels cost too much for a couple of dirty mattresses in a small, airless room. The police would be checking the bus station. I decided we'd spend the rest of the night outside. I looked and looked, dragging Elena after me. I finally settled on a portico jutting out from one end of the *mercado*. I wasn't the only one with this idea. There were others sleeping here. At least we wouldn't be alone.

I didn't ask Elena's opinion, and she didn't offer one. I hoped she spent the worst night of her life. And, for the hundredth time since leaving San Jacinto, I wished I didn't have a sister.

CHAPTER 16

I sat with my back against the only column in the portico not already claimed by another migrant. Even that late at night, the humidity was dense. The mildewed wall felt cold and clammy through my shirt. Chips of dirty white paint littered the ground, mingled with scraps of metal, discarded food wrappers, a doll's head.

Elena spread out her shawl, curled up, and put her head on my leg. She let out one loud yawn and, within seconds, fell into a deep sleep.

Next to us was a dented, rusted-out oil drum. The stink of old urine crept around from the other side of the barrel. No wonder no one else had chosen this spot. My right leg had already fallen asleep under the weight of Elena's head. I sighed and tried to stretch out my free left leg. We couldn't afford to oversleep, anyway. The bus left at six in the morning.

A feeble street lamp cast a dim light into the first few feet of the portico. One couple, their arms around each other, whispered quietly. A drunk lay in the far corner. He mumbled nonstop to himself. At least ten others slept in the shadows cast by the columns. Most of them, again, were men, alone.

A rat strolled across the portico, taking its time. Three or four others followed, their long tails stuck out behind them. The rats didn't seem afraid of us humans. This was their home. Had I really looked hard enough for a place to sleep? Anywhere would have been better than this.

Another rat ran right over Elena's shoe. Maybe the rats were a bad omen. I was dead tired, but I needed to stay awake. There was more than one kind of *ratero* in the world.

I touched the money pouch strapped to my waist. I needed

every *peso* to take us home, to pay off Juanito, to perhaps, if I was lucky, start my trip all over. I pulled up my shirt, took off the pouch, and stuffed it behind the barrel. It would be safe there until morning. The stink would keep everyone away. The only thing I had to do was stay awake.

An hour passed, then another. Elena didn't move. The rats came and went. I counted them. I named them: Juanito, Juanito I, Juanito II, Morales, Morales I, Morales II. I made up stories about them. In every one, the rats died horrible, gory deaths. I slapped my face and pinched my arm, really hard. I tried to remember every soccer game I'd ever played, in order, and the scores.

I listed the kids in my class, first alphabetically, then by their height, then by how *mensos* they were. There were the dumb ones, and then there were the ones that just acted dumb. I lined them up both ways.

I thought again about how angry I was with Elena, how she'd messed up everything. Even that didn't work to keep me awake. My eyes closed, again and again. I looked around the portico, into the darkness of the shadows. All I could hear was scurrying paws and the soft snoring of someone across the open space. Rats or no rats, I was dead tired. We'd have to get up soon, anyway. For sure I'd wake up at the littlest sound. It wouldn't hurt to sleep for a few minutes, would it?

A vicious kick in my side jolted me awake. I groaned in pain, and rolled over to see Elena sitting up straight, her eyes wide with terror. Two figures hovered over me, their faces hidden by the shadow of a column.

"Wake up," one growled.

I couldn't see them clearly, but I saw the gun pointed at Elena's head. They jerked her roughly to her feet. Before I could stand, another kick landed squarely in my stomach. I doubled over in pain, grabbing my middle.

"What do you want?" I gasped. But I knew what they wanted. These muggers probably came through here every night, taking whatever they could find.

No one answered my question. Instead, they pushed me to the ground again. Rough hands moved quickly up and down my body. The hands pulled Chuy's knife from my right pocket, along with the few *pesos* not in the pouch.

The thief dug through my backpack, then threw it aside. The only thing he took was Lalo's soccer jersey. He fingered the shiny fabric, then put it on. The shirt was now his. He rooted through Elena's string bag, opened the purse full of letters, and dumped them on the ground. He balled up the little cloth purse in disgust and threw it out into the darkness. Then he kicked at the letters, and ground several of them with his heel into the earth. Elena groaned, as if she'd been kicked herself.

"There's nothing here, Colmillo. *No tienen nada,*" he said with disdain. He gave me another half-hearted kick in the thigh.

Colmillo moved into the light. He had acne, a bad case of it. Deep scars and pockmarks covered his whole face. A new set of pimples ran across his nose and cheeks, leaking yellow pus. A scraggly, thin moustache covered his upper lip. He wanted it to make him look older. It didn't work.

Colmillo was a kid, like me. A boy, *un baboso,* had tied up my sister and put a gun to her head. How could I have let this happen?

I started to get up again, angry at myself then. This time, Colmillo let me stand. I felt his partner behind me, his bad breath on my neck, so close I could smell the rancid sweat from his armpits. I looked around for help, but the portico was empty. Everyone had either been robbed or scared off.

"Well, it doesn't matter." Colmillo grinned meanly.

Then I saw the source of his nickname. A shiny gold canine tooth glinted in the light of the street lamp. Colmillo ran one finger lightly over Elena's cheek. She looked small, like a child. Her eyelids fluttered rapidly, then shut. Her knees gave way, and she slipped to the ground in a little heap.

A deep, terrible dread washed through every part of my body.

"Wait! Please wait! I have money . . . ," I said.

The man behind me snorted, but Colmillo squinted his eyes in interest. He'd seen desperation before. He'd gotten money from it before—probably lots of money.

"Really," I pleaded. "Let us go. I'll get it."

"There," I nodded my head in the direction of the oil drum. "Look behind the barrel, you'll find it. Take it all. Just leave us alone."

Colmillo motioned with the gun. His partner searched with one hand, pulled out the money pouch, and then the bills. He held them out for Colmillo to see and counted them quickly.

Colmillo's eyebrows raised in surprise. It was more than he expected. He reached for the pouch and stuffed it into his pocket. This time he'd settle for quick, easy money.

"Quita a estos piojosos de aquí," Colmillo sneered. "Sometimes it's just so easy, it's not even fun."

His partner threw me to the ground next to Elena. Their footsteps, and their laughter, echoed across the portico. We'd been easy marks. I rolled over and threw up. We'd lost our bus tickets and all of our money. Chuy's knife, Lalo's jersey, both gone. How much worse could things get?

CHAPTER 17

"I'm ready to give up, Elena."

I groaned, then leaned over and picked up my backpack, now completely empty, and tucked it under my arm.

"Maybe this trip just wasn't meant to be."

Elena didn't answer. She pulled herself up to her hands and knees and looked at Mamá's letters scattered across the portico. A breeze had caught several and sent them out into the gutter. She picked up the one closest to her, blew the dirt off the paper, and looked at the words scrawled across the page. She held the letter open in both palms, like an offering, then let it drift back down to the ground.

Her eyes searched around in the dim light. She bent closer, and then got down on her hands and the tips of her toes, moving like a crab across the dirt, her face close to the ground, examining every square centimeter as she went.

Elena seemed to be looking for a particular letter, one that held special meaning for her. But she ignored each and every one she came across. Finally, she stooped even lower and picked up something from the ground.

"Gracias a Dios," she murmured. She stood and walked unsteadily toward me. In her hands was the cloth purse that had held Mamá's letters.

"Come on, Miguel. Let's get out of here." She looked around nervously. There was no sign of Colmillo. There was no sign of anyone. Even the rats had disappeared.

"Let me help you with these." I picked up one letter close to my shoe, folded it along its well-creased lines, and held it out to Elena to stow in the bag. The letters seemed important to *me* now. They were the only things we had left.

"Forget them, Miguel. *¡Olvídalo!* Please, let's just go. Please!" Elena reached down for my hand, to help me up. It was already hot out, but her hand was cold and clammy.

I groaned as I rose to my feet. Every part of me hurt. "Are you sure, Elena?" I asked. "The letters—"

"We have to get out of here," Elena cut me off. Elena must have been scared to death by Colmillo. What else would make her leave her precious letters?

She steered me out of the portico, and out into the street. Dawn would come soon. The barest hint of light was visible to the east, and the sky had turned a deep blue. We turned the corner and entered the far side of the *mercado,* cutting behind to the row of stalls where we first hid from Morales.

A few farmers who'd come in to sell their mangos and chiles unloaded their goods from the backs of burros. They looked at us curiously, then went back to their work. I looked down at my filthy, torn clothes. We probably looked like fugitives. The farmers would be better off if they pretended they'd never seen us.

"*Aquí,*" said Elena. She sat down on the ground in the very place where I'd taken the money she'd gotten from Juanito.

Elena turned the cloth purse inside out and put it up to her mouth. She tore at the silky purple lining with her teeth, again and again, trying to find a spot that would give way. A small tear finally appeared at one seam, now soaked with Elena's saliva. She lowered the bag, put one index finger in the tear, and ripped the lining apart. A cascade of bills fell out of the purse, onto Elena's lap. She gathered them up and put them in my hands.

"This is the other half of the money Juanito gave me." Big tears rolled down Elena's cheeks. For once, she had good reason to cry. She had a thousand good reasons to cry.

"I sewed it into the lining here, just in case." She pulled her knees up to her chin, and hid her face.

"*¡Embustera!*" I said, looking at the little treasure in my hands.

Elena had been tricky. She'd lied to me about how much money Juanito had given her, but she'd taken the precaution of hiding half of it.

"I'll go back home, Miguel. I'll go back by myself and you go on ahead." She dried her tears with the back of one dirty hand. "Maybe there's still enough money for you, if you're careful."

She was solemn. She wasn't whining. She meant it.

I looked at my sister hard. Despite everything she'd done wrong, she'd won my admiration. I even admired her sneakiness. She'd done everything without giving herself away. I'd never had a clue about her intentions, not one of them.

Then together, we'd escaped Morales and Colmillo, by the skin of our teeth. Whatever we did, we had to do it as brother and sister. We'd been through too much to separate now. If Elena went to San Jacinto, I'd go too. If I went north, I'd take her with me. Still, there wasn't enough money to pay the *coyote* for both of us. We needed help.

"Look, Elena. I think we should call Papá and Mamá. They'll be worried, anyway. And, if worse comes to worse, we could ask Don Clemente for more money," I said. I didn't tell her that he'd give us all the money we wanted. All we had to do was ask.

Elena looked down at her nails. They were chewed down so badly that several were bleeding. She knew she'd be in trouble for following me. But she nodded silently in agreement. So we made our way to the bus station, got a large pile of coins, and stood close together next to the pay phone.

I dialed the California phone number, Elena pumped in the coins, and the phone rang. It rang and rang and rang. A weary, unfamiliar female voice finally answered. No, Papá and Mamá didn't live there anymore. Yes, they'd moved. No, she didn't know the new number.

Elena and I looked at each other, unsurprised. The family had to move too often—and often unexpectedly. Abuelita, one way or another, would have the new number. But Abuelita had no phone.

"Try Don Clemente," Elena suggested. "Maybe Papá called him with their new number."

Don Clemente's private number was first on the list of important information I'd memorized. "Do not call unless you must," had been written in his own hand. I nodded and dialed.

"*Hola.* Who's calling?" demanded a familiar voice.

What was Juanito doing with Don Clemente's phone? I wanted to hang up right then. I wanted to tell Juanito I knew what he was up to when he lent Elena money. I wanted to tell him to go and screw himself.

Instead, I just said, "Let me talk to Don Clemente. It's Miguel."

A silence followed. "Juanito, are you there? Are you there?" I asked.

I thought I heard him chuckle. "What do you want, Miguel? I thought *mi tío* gave you everything you needed."

"Just put him on. I need to ask him something." I wouldn't give Juanito the satisfaction of knowing what had happened to me, to us.

"Well, you'll have to ask me now." Juanito's voice was calm and cold.

"What do you mean?" I asked, but I didn't want to know the answer.

Juanito didn't answer. He let the silence hang on the line.

"Don Clemente is dead," he finally answered. "A traffic accident. Somehow his Mercedes went off the road up on the mountain. It was tragic, really, a freak sort of thing." He didn't sound like he thought it was a tragedy.

"So, naturally, I'm now in charge of his operation, all of his networks. The *coyotes,* the *polleros,* the merchandise—everything. If you want something, you'll have to ask me. And I'm replacing his people with mine, with those loyal to me."

I didn't answer. I hung the phone on the hook quietly. With this conversation, the road back to San Jacinto was closed. I couldn't let

Elena return by herself. She already owed Juanito money. He might decide that she owed him more than that. We had to go north with no clear plans and no help we could count on.

I took the money and split it right down the middle—half for Elena, half for me. I couldn't pretend I was her boss anymore. We bought food and a run-down hotel room for one night.

Elena sat on the edge of the sagging mattress and carefully sewed her money back into the lining of the bag. I could hide mine on my body. There was at least one good place. But who was I kidding? If someone wanted it, they'd find it, no matter where I stuck it.

The only thing I had left from the beginning of my trip was Abuelita's *Virgen de Guadalupe* medallion. With everything that had happened, I'd forgotten all about it. I took it off and inspected the links in the chain, one by one. A couple of Abuelita's hairs still clung stubbornly to the necklace, as if part of her refused to be separated from *La Virgencita*.

Abuelita believed in *La Virgen*'s powers of protection and guidance. I just believed in Abuelita. I checked the clasp and put the medallion back around my neck. It had seemed featherlight before, but now the cool, smooth metal felt solid and weighty against my chest.

CHAPTER 18

They called it the *mata gente,* the "people killer." It was an ordinary freight train that passed through once a day, and it was the one way to get north without paying a *peso*. It had oil cars, rounded, sleek and shiny, and open hopper cars carrying grain or scrap metal. Ladders ran halfway up the sides of the faded orange, yellow, and brown cargo cars.

It was simple, they said. As the train slowed, you ran alongside, grabbed one of the ladders, and hopped on.

Fácil. Everyone told us how easy it was to hop on board the train. And everyone told us about the unlucky ones who didn't make it. The ones who survived were all over town, broken and abandoned, but still living. They were everywhere.

One, a woman they called Angelita, sat outside the shabby clinic, telling her story to anyone who would listen. The train had cut off both of her legs midthigh when she lost her grip and fell beneath the wheels. She would have died if two others hadn't jumped off to drag her from beneath the train and stop the blood flowing from her limbs.

Another, called Santos, wheeled himself clumsily through the *zócalo,* begging for money so he could return to his family in Honduras. He was paralyzed from the waist down and all four fingers of his right hand were gone. They said that Santos was pushed off the train. Someone wanted his place on a ladder that already held five others.

"We're going to hop the *mata gente* anyway," I declared to Elena.

We watched Santos steer his wheelchair toward the bus station. There were always people there willing to give up a *peso* or two, out of guilt. They were getting out of here. Santos had to stay.

"Okay, Miguel. We're young and fast, right Miguel?" Elena added. "Maybe Santos was just too slow, or something."

I didn't remind her that we had no choice.

We walked to the train yard in the early evening. A gentle breeze lifted up some scattered papers. Halfway there, Elena skipped, then hopped, then showed me just once how fast she could run.

"See? See, Miguel?" she said. "I can do it!"

"I know!" I yelled to her. "*¡Sí se puede!* We will, Elena!"

Things had changed between us. I knew how it felt to be *macho,* to try to boss Elena around, to ignore her, to fight with her, like I did in San Jacinto. Things felt different now, since Morales, since Colmillo and Juanito.

We crossed through the yard littered with sidetracked, broken-down freight cars. I put my ear down on a track to listen for the train, the way Chuy and Lalo and I used to do in San Jacinto. The hot fat metal rail held no clues.

I crawled up into one of the cars and pulled Elena up after me. Its big doors gaped open, and we sat with our legs dangling down. From here we could see the *mata gente* coming. We'd have time to position ourselves and to get ready.

In the near distance, a small group was making its way into the train yard. One of them pointed and gestured and moved his body along a track as if he was shadowing a moving train. He loped, picked up speed, and grabbed an imaginary ladder. And then I heard a familiar voice, talking nonstop to the others.

"See, this is how you do it," he instructed. "You just run and then hop right on!"

"Look who's here, Miguel!" Elena yelled, jumping down. "Come on!"

Within seconds, Javier had Elena in a giant *abrazo*. He reached out to pull me into the circle. I felt myself resist, but Elena grabbed my waist and tugged me in closer. We made a triangle, Javi and Elena the base, me floating loosely at the top.

"I knew I'd see you again. It is fate, really," Javi said.

Javi's companions, a young couple, the woman pregnant, smiled at the reunion. Then they turned around and left, going back the way they came.

"They're scared of the train. I told them what to do, but who knows? Maybe they'll try, maybe they won't," Javier said in one breath.

"Good thing you're leaving. I'm glad to get out of here myself," he continued. "Morales stuck me in jail for a day. He never figured out I tricked him. Then he put me on the other side of the river. But, just like I told you, here I am, again."

Javi seemed happy, even joyful, about tricking Morales and making it back. But his eyes were red, and his face was drawn. He hadn't slept, I could see that.

Within seconds, Javi put himself in charge. He took each of us by an arm and propelled us down the train tracks. "We'll get the train down there."

He pointed beyond the end of the yard toward the dense underbrush. "It's better. I've checked it out already. The *federales* swing through the train yard every now and then."

We followed the tracks for several hundred meters. The grass on both sides was firmly packed down, evidence that many train-hoppers had waited here before us. In the thick undergrowth beyond the grass, others had cut back the brush to make places to sleep, or to hide. A dead campfire blackened the ground in one spot. A faint wisp of smoke crept up from the center.

A pack of yellow-eyed dogs emerged from the brush and wandered toward us, sniffing the ground. The leader eyed us boldly. I picked up a rock and flung it in his direction. Javi ran after the dogs, screaming, "Go on! Get out of here! *¡Lárguense de aquí!*" I hoped the dogs weren't like the rats, another bad omen.

CHAPTER 19

Javi chose a spot just before the track curved for us to wait. "This is good," he declared. "The *mata gente* will still be going slow enough for us to hop on. It'll be here in less than an hour. You'll see, no problem. But first things first."

From his pack, he took out a pocketknife, the kind with miniature tools attached. He pulled out the little scissors from one side and held them out to Elena.

"You need to cut your hair off, all off, short. Then put your cap back on," Javi instructed.

He looked away, but continued, "You should disguise yourself. The less you look like a girl, the better. There are train gangs. They rob, steal, beat people up. . . ."

Javi paused. Finally, he looked back at Elena. "And they rape many women."

The look I saw in Elena's eyes when Colmillo robbed us returned for just a moment. She grabbed the scissors and began to hack away at her hair. It fell to the ground in dark, thick clumps. She cut and cut her hair. Then she asked Javi to cut it even more, until it lay like a small black cap on her head.

When he finished, Javi stood with the little scissors open in his hand, staring at Elena. "You look like *m'ija* Magdalena with your hair like that. She cut it short herself last year. She plays soccer, climbs trees, runs. She said she didn't want to bother with her hair. Really, you could be *hermanas,* you look so much like her."

Javi seemed unable to move. He seemed stuck to the ground. He couldn't take his eyes off Elena's face.

"What else, Javi? What else?" Elena demanded.

She just wanted to finish. She just wanted to get it over with. Elena looked down at her clothes. Her pants and loose shirt, her sneakers—all of them could've belonged to a boy. It looked like a good disguise to me. With her cap pulled down over her eyes, she would fool almost anybody.

Javi turned, and dug into his backpack. He pulled out a black marker and handed it to me. His hand trembled. He looked me in the eye, but it seemed he was looking straight through me to a place a long ways away.

"Write '*Tengo SIDA*' in big letters across her chest," he said quietly. "The threat of AIDS might stop some men."

I swallowed hard, took the top off the marker, and wrote the words in thick block letters right above Elena's small breasts. It was warm, but she shivered anyway. I shivered, too, at all the things I didn't know, and didn't want to know.

And how could I protect Elena when I didn't have a clue about all the things I was supposed to protect her from?

Of course Javi had a plan for getting on the train. He made us run through the steps ten times before he was satisfied. I didn't see why we had to practice hopping the *mata gente*. We were young and quick and there was no one else around to fight us for a spot on a ladder.

"It's coming!" Javi said. "Can you hear it?" At that moment, the *mata gente*'s whistle blew loudly. It was close, very close.

"Come on! Get in position!" Javi demanded. We lined up, Elena in front. We began trotting along the tracks, eyes on the cross ties to avoid tripping.

Suddenly, the *mata gente* came roaring up, a giant creature with whirling steel wheels. It was moving much faster than I'd imagined it would, and we would have just one chance to make it on.

"Elena! Elena!" My voice was swallowed up by the noise of the beast. "Faster. *¡Más rápido!*"

I glanced backward over my shoulder. Javier was right behind me. "Get the first one you can!" I yelled to Elena.

Elena ran even faster and, in one motion, leaped at the lowest rung of a freight car ladder. She hung on with one hand, turned, and shouted, "Miguel! Miguel, come on!"

She held out her free hand. The *mata gente* was picking up speed, fast. For a moment, I imagined Elena fading into the distance. I saw myself tripping and falling, dragged into the stomach of the monster. It ate me up and I felt nothing.

"Go, Miguel," Javier puffed in my ear. "Now!"

From somewhere I found the speed I needed. I grabbed the rung with one hand, Elena's hand with the other. We moved up the ladder and, somehow, Javi attached himself below us.

The train rounded the corner and then, from the bushes, from the grass, dozens and dozens of people began to throw themselves at the *mata gente*. They ran and pushed and shoved. A few ended up like us, clinging to a ladder. The others were like a swarm of pesky flies. The *mata gente* just swatted them away and moved forward.

The young couple, Javi's friends from the train yard, ran clumsily along. The husband urged his pregnant wife to go faster. She never had a chance. They crumpled together onto their knees next to the track.

A thin little boy scrambled easily up a ladder, only to lose his grip suddenly. He fell like a leaf, silently.

An old man with watery desperate eyes looked like he would make it. But, at the last moment, just as he reached for Javi's extended fingers, the tip of his cowboy boot caught on a railroad tie. He tripped, stumbled, and disappeared without a sound beneath the grinding wheels.

It was over as fast as it began. Within seconds, the train moved beyond the unlucky ones. Javi, Elena, and I crawled numbly to the top of the car and lay down flat, Elena in the middle. Javi cried quietly. The roar of the *mata gente* turned to a rhythmic low rumble. We held hands and turned our bodies toward the front of the train, facing north.

CHAPTER 20

The sun set, the moon rose, and the *mata gente* moved us steadily along. Javi took a length of rope from his pack, lashed us together through our belt loops, and secured the rope to a rail on top of the car. Javi made us as safe as he could, but he did it grimly. The *mata gente* had sucked out all of his good humor.

The other *mata gente* hoppers, most of them young, children really, perched on the cars in front of us, like little birds on a limb riding out a storm. The cars swayed side to side. They rocked and jolted and lurched. We settled into the crazy rhythm, unable to talk. It was too hard to hear. Words traveled back with the wind from the car ahead, only to be swallowed up by the clatter of the wheels.

"No train gangs so far," Javi spoke into my ear. "Rest some. I'll keep watch for a while."

I lay down and watched the progress of the moon across the starry sky. For hours I drifted in and out of sleep atop the roaring train. Javi thought we could make it more than halfway to the border on the *mata gente*, maybe farther if we were lucky. I thought it was about time we had some good luck.

I woke up for the third time when the moon had descended almost to the horizon. The train's brakes screeched. The large jolt threw me toward the front of the car. The train slowed to a crawl. Javi frowned and untied himself from our rope. He climbed partway down the ladder on the side of the car and leaned out as far as he could.

"I can't see what's going on up there." Javi motioned toward the engine. "Can you see anything from the top?"

We stood up. People ran along the tops of the cars toward us, leaping across the chasms between the cars. Others scrambled down the side ladders as fast as they could.

A warning echoed from car to car. "*¡La migra!* Get off! Run!"

We climbed quickly down our ladder and jumped off the train. We ran into a thick grove of trees, then turned around and watched, ready to plunge farther into the forest. The *migra* made a show of rounding up the slowest ones but didn't bother to try to find the rest. By the time the train started up again, they had left, and we were back in our place on top.

For the next two days, the *mata gente* was home. Five more times we jumped off to avoid capture by *la migra*. Once we even got off, skirted around a small town, and hopped on once again on the other side. Javi said the *migra* had a checkpoint in the dead center of town. I don't know how, but each time, Javier seemed to know what we should do.

But by evening of the second day, we'd had only sips of water from one bottle and two small *bolillos* to share. We were hungry, but mostly we were dead tired. Even when we could stay on top of our car, we could never rest.

Two boys got swept off the car right in front of us by a low-hanging branch. They fell into a ditch full of dirty brown water. We had to duck again and again to avoid electrical wires. If we touched one, we'd die, just like that. The metal rails, hot from the sun, burned our hands. We coughed up the diesel smoke that filled our lungs.

"I can't go on," Elena finally yelled above the roar of the engine. "I need to eat something. I need to drink. I want a bed!"

Dark circles of fatigue ringed Elena's eyes. Her face was streaked with diesel soot and she blew diesel snot out of her runny nose. Her jeans were stained and torn at the knees. Her lower lip trembled.

"Don't worry," Javi called back. "I've heard that up ahead there are some people who take care of migrants like us. We'll get some food."

Elena shook her head in disbelief. "Fairy tales are for little girls," she screamed above the roar of the train. " I don't believe in *el hada madrina* anymore. I hate this stupid train!"

The brakes squealed and the train slowed, again. If we had to hop off and on here, just one more time, one of us wouldn't make it. One of us would not have the strength. Right now, it was a toss-up between Elena and Javier. I hadn't seen Javi rest at all. He'd been awake, vigilant, looking out for every big and little danger. How much sleep could he do without, anyway?

The train whistle blew three times. The *mata gente* slowed even more, but did not stop. Javi moved toward the edge of the car.

Elena shook her head again. "I'm getting off here and I'm not getting back on."

And then I saw people gathered at the side of the tracks. They were throwing things at the train, probably rocks or bricks. Maybe they hated migrants like us in this *pueblito*. We flattened our bodies on top of the car. But nothing fell on us. Instead, I heard a girl, two cars ahead of us, laughing.

I peeked over the side of the car. There, running alongside, was a fit middle-aged man.

"Here!" he yelled, keeping pace with the *mata gente*. "Catch!"

More people swarmed from their houses, their arms full. They aimed and threw and they didn't miss. They'd done this before, lots of times.

I reached out my arms and caught a plastic-wrapped package of tortillas. An old woman held out a water bottle full to the brim, a young girl a plastic bag with fruit. Javi leaned from the ladder and grabbed both.

A whole bagful of bread landed in Elena's outstretched hands. At the bottom was some ham. Everyone on the top of the train got gifts: loaves of bread, lemonade, sandwiches, even sweaters and blankets.

All up and down the train, the *migrantes* yelled down, "*¡Gracias! ¡Gracias!*"

"*¡Dios los proteja!*" the people on the ground called back.

But there were some who held nothing in their hands. One old woman stood unsteadily, too close to the moving train. Our eyes met.

"Go to your father," she urged.

Another old man called out, over and over, "Find your mothers."

The people of this *pueblito* knew the *mata gente* was full of boys and girls, just kids. Just like Elena. Just like me. The people knew we were looking for our *padres* and *madres*. There must be trainload after trainload of *niños*, all of them headed north, searching for their families.

Javi didn't smile at the *bendiciones* from below. He looked haunted, as if a ghost had just whispered into his ear. Well, no wonder. He was, after all, the one doing the leaving. His own children would be forced to hop the *mata gente* someday, if they ever wanted to see him again. They could die from a train gang, or thirst or hunger, or just pure loneliness.

I looked at Javi again. How many times would he make promises to *his* children back in El Salvador, promises he couldn't keep once he got to his brother in New York?

Then it wasn't Javi I saw. Instead, it was Papá. Papá's face was exactly as it was the day he left me. Papá left without me. *Me abandonó.* He could've taken me with him and he didn't. Or he could've stayed, just stayed, and made it work in San Jacinto. Or, he could've snapped a finger, and just like magic, Don Clemente would have sent me.

So there we were, Elena and I, making that trip. *¿Y para qué?* How many times had we already escaped death, or worse? And we hadn't even reached the border yet.

Well, I'd been only partly alive anyway, for a long time. Papá took a big part of me with him to California when he left. He thought he was sending for me now, but I'd already been there and he didn't even know it.

I searched for a word to describe how I felt at that moment, but I realized I felt nothing for Papá. *Nada, absolutamente nada.* Where there should have been feeling, there was just a big black hole of emptiness.

CHAPTER 21

The train rounded a curve and slowed to a crawl. The whistle sounded twice. The *mata gente* chugged forward, then stopped next to a tall water tower. Several figures leaped from the tower, onto the *mata gente* two cars in front of us.

"It's a train gang." Javi grabbed Elena's hand. "Follow me, quickly."

We scrambled down the ladder between the cars and ran toward a small group of buildings, away from the water tower, on the opposite side of the train.

"Here," Javi wheezed. He pulled us behind a corrugated metal shed. We knelt and peeked through the ragged holes of the rusted-out walls. Javi sat cross-legged, coughed deeply, then spit black saliva on the ground. He stuffed his head into his arms to muffle two or three more coughs. In between coughs, he breathed heavily.

The gang dragged three young girls off the train, screaming and begging to be let go. They disappeared into the bushes on the far side of the water tower. Elena shrank down to the ground, pulled her cap down tight over her head, and hugged her knees.

"Come on, Elena, we've got to get back on. Come on. We'll miss the train," I urged.

I grabbed her elbows, now locked firmly around her legs. I tugged, and Elena's whole body moved in response. She was a tight little ball of fear. Javi pushed himself to his feet. He pried one of Elena's hands loose from around her knees, held it in his callused palm, and gently straightened each stiff finger one by one.

"I won't let anything happen to you," Javi huffed. "You'll make it across *la línea*, all the way north. I swear to you on my life. *Lo juro*." We'd been quiet for many minutes, but he breathed as if he hadn't stopped running.

Elena said nothing, but she let Javi lead her by the hand back to the train and boost her up.

After that, Elena wouldn't take her eyes off Javi. She looked at him as if he held the secrets to the whole universe. I could read her mind: Javi had saved us—all of us—from Morales. He'd been right about how to hop the *mata gente*. He was right about the people from *el pueblito* with the food and about the train gangs.

And then, not half an hour later, the *mata gente* screeched to a halt. I leaned out to see why we'd stopped, yet again. Ahead, I saw the lowered bars of a railroad crossing, and stretched across the tracks, their weapons drawn, a cadre of soldiers with weapons.

"Jump!" Javi screamed. Elena hurried down the ladder and leaped onto the gravel by the track. I followed quickly, with Javi right behind. I landed squarely on both feet, but Javi cried out in pain the moment he hit the ground. I turned to see him roll in the dirt, grabbing his right ankle.

"Go on!" Javi's face was screwed up in agony. "Run! Get out of here!"

I looked up the tracks. The other train hoppers were scurrying down the sides of the train in swarms. Already I could see those at the front raising their arms above their heads in defeat. We were at the back of the train. There was a small chance we could escape.

Javi continued his pleas. "You have time. Go now!"

But Elena and I each grabbed one arm and pulled him up. "Lean on me!" I demanded.

We hobbled together toward a cornfield, and began to make our way down a row. At first all I could hear was the dim echo of the *mata gente* still roaring in my ears. But then I caught the sound of the soldiers running down the tracks, their boots crunching on the rocky railroad bed.

One yelled, "*¡El fil!* I saw some go into the field!"

We cut to the right. Every few steps, Javi pleaded with us to leave him. I got ready to surrender. If they caught us, if we had to go back home, Elena and I wouldn't do it all over again. As for Javi, he couldn't. He'd never make it.

Again we cut right, through the cornstalks grown higher than our heads. I couldn't see what lay beyond the field, but I led us in a diagonal direction, toward where I thought the field ended. Javi put as much weight as he could on his left foot to lessen our burden, but each time his right foot grazed the ground, he groaned. Elena and I half carried him, half dragged him. His body was solid and muscled and heavy.

Behind us, the soldiers crashed through the corn, cursing. We reached the edge of the field. To the left, a series of low hills rose quickly to a low peak covered in clouds. Bright green coffee plants covered the terraced ground as far as the eye could see.

In front of us, a dense tangle of vines appeared to lead into a thick grove of plantains. I pushed through the first layer, pulling the vines apart with my hands. I went back for Elena and Javier, then attacked the next layer in front of us. We had to bend down to get through. Javi crawled on his hands and knees. On the other side of the thicket of vines, we paused to catch our breath.

I looked behind us. "Shhh!" I cautioned to Javi and Elena.

We strained to hear our pursuers. We didn't move. We barely breathed. But there was no sound of the soldiers or the train.

"They've given up," Javi whispered. "Incompetence . . . or laziness. We're not worth the effort. They probably got their quota, anyway."

He sat up and pushed his bad right ankle out in front of him. He clenched his teeth, unlaced his boot, and teased it off his foot. It had been only minutes, but already the ankle was puffy.

Javi touched the ankle carefully with his forefinger. "I won't be able to walk on this for a couple of days, at least."

He didn't look up at us. "You two need to go back the way we came. Get the next train that comes through," Javi said quietly.

Javi wouldn't be able to help us now. In fact, he would be an obstacle. What should we do now? Should Elena and I go on, like Javi said? Who knew how long it might take for him to be well enough to travel?

And if we had to walk across the desert? Then what? He'd slow us down, for sure. Elena and I could hop back on the train and save the rest of our money.

Javi was right. It was time for Elena and me to go it alone again. It was the only way.

CHAPTER 22

"No!" Elena exclaimed. "I'm not leaving Javi!" She glared at me. She knew what I was thinking.

Elena's face was diesel-streaked, her short hair stuck out from her head in uneven, greasy spikes, her "boy" clothes hung torn and filthy from her skinny body. She put her dirty right index finger to her mouth and chewed at what was left of the nail.

The chances of me changing her mind were zero. She wouldn't leave Javier, not after the train gang.

"I'm going to see if I can find us some water," I announced. I needed to get away. I needed to be alone, to think.

I grabbed Javi's water bottle and headed away from the little clearing toward a trail that disappeared into the forest. Thousands of birds sang and called in the forest canopy above my head, the first natural sounds I'd heard since the roar of the *mata gente* had filled my ears.

I finally found a small but swiftly moving stream. I filled the water bottle, drank deeply, filled it again, then collapsed on the pebbled bank.

What else could we do to get the rest of the way north? Try to find work? Hah! Doing what? Who would hire a couple of dirty teenagers or an old man, anyway? I couldn't get work even in San Jacinto where everyone knew me.

If we had to, we could beg. Yes, there was always begging. I tried to picture myself with my hand out or knocking on a stranger's door, eyes downcast, hunched over to look smaller. Even so, the most we could hope for from begging was a little food. Nobody around here had money to hand out. No, hopping back on the *mata gente* was our only real choice.

I trudged toward the clearing, one slow step at a time. How

could I talk some sense into Elena? But before I broke through the brush, I heard the voices of strangers. The soldiers hadn't given up after all! They'd found us!

I crouched and peered through the branches. At first, all I could see was what seemed to be the back end of a burro and a pair of gnarled bare feet. I inched closer. These were no soldiers.

I pushed my way back through the thicket and stood next to Elena. In her hands was her little cloth bag. This time it had been cut open with Javi's knife. An old Indian man nodded slowly and tucked some of Elena's *pesos* away under his shirt. An old Indian woman, her silver braids swinging behind her, reached into a pack tied to the burro, took out a package, and handed it to Javi. Without a word, they plodded slowly away.

"We have a ride," Javi announced. "Their Spanish isn't so good, but we managed. A *primo* drives a truck. He's going north tomorrow, and he'll let us ride in back."

"How could you do this without talking to me first? We need every *peso*, you know that. How could you?" I demanded.

"I knew you'd say no. Besides, it's the only way we'll make it." Elena stuck out her chin and crossed her arms.

I grabbed Elena's elbow and dragged her to the far side of the clearing.

"No, Elena," I answered through clenched teeth. "It's the only way *he'll* make it. It's the only way Javier will make it."

I stared at Javi. He started to open the packet of food. He tugged at the string around the package. He didn't look at me, or Elena.

"He's just using us, Elena. *¿No lo puedes ver? ¿Estás ciega?* He's only thinking what's best for him. *He* needs a ride. *We* don't."

Elena probably thought she was being loyal, but Javi would leave us if he had to, wouldn't he? Wouldn't he do whatever he had to do, so he could make it for his family? Isn't that what a *real* father would do, put his own family first? Elena was just too young to understand.

"You just can't stand it, Miguel. You can't stand to have me be right. You're so used to Abuelita just thinking you're so great, that you can do no wrong. The money was mine, anyway. It was *mine*. Yours got stolen by Colmillo, remember?"

"*Cállate,* Elena. Why don't *you* see the truth for a change?" I snapped back.

Elena didn't back down. She looked me straight in the eye, just the way she looked at the goat before she hit it right on the head.

"Or better yet, ask *him* what to do!" I pointed at Javi. "You seem to think he has all the answers. Well, ask *him* how we get a *coyote* with no money! Ask *him* how we're going to get across the border!"

"I have to ask Javi, don't I? He saved us from Morales, didn't he? You didn't know how to get us on the *mata gente*, or about the train gangs. At least he got us a ride all the way to the border. You didn't *know* anything. You didn't *do* anything!"

Elena moved up closer. She was small, but she stood toe-to-toe with me.

"I used to lie awake at night in San Jacinto and pretend that Papá and Mamá came home to get us," Elena went on, her voice quiet, but fierce. "Sometimes I even pretended they came home to stay.

"When I finally gave up on that, I pretended that you'd take me across *la línea*. You'd be the one, Miguel, you. I thought I could count on you."

"Grow up, Elena." Neither of us had moved. "Guess what? You want to hear something? Don Clemente told me he'd have sent us years ago to Papá and Mamá, but Papá wouldn't hear of it. He wouldn't take a *peso*, not even for us."

Elena stepped back. She looked like I'd hit her full on, right in the mouth.

"You had to read Mamá's letters instead of having her there, right there, in front of you, all because of Papá's stupid pride.

"Do you get it, Elena? We never needed to wait. You never needed to pretend anything."

She'd hurt me as much as she could. I'd just hurt her back, because *I* could, because I was tired of her, of Javi, of everything— because I was tired of carrying the big load Don Clemente had dumped on me about Papá.

I turned away from my sister and picked up my backpack. Elena didn't think she needed me. Any idea I'd had about us being a team had vanished.

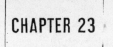

CHAPTER 23

"I don't believe you, Miguel. You're just saying that about Papá, just to make me feel bad." Elena moved again in front of me.

"Mamá wouldn't have let that happen. She wouldn't have." Elena spoke to herself then, not to me, as if she was trying to convince herself it was true. Mamá was *her* savior, just as I'd always thought Papá was mine.

"Believe what you want. Do what you want, Elena," I finally said. "You always do, anyway."

I could give in to Javi and Elena's plan. It was two against one. She looked up to Javi. She trusted him, like a *tío* or godfather, maybe even a father. All we had left now was part of Juanito's money. Javi would probably find a reason to use the rest of it up, and Elena would just go along with him. Well, not me.

I began to walk away, back into the forest. "Go with Javi. I'm hopping back on the train, tomorrow if I can. Maybe I'll see you at the border. Or California."

Elena's face fell. "Miguel, I didn't mean—," she began.

I cut her off. "If you change your mind, I'll be camped close to the train tracks."

I found my way back to the stream. I bent and started to wash the first layer of diesel stink and grime from the train off my body. I used the small pebbles from the bottom of the stream to scrub my skin. I smelled my hands and wrinkled my nose. I stunk. Even if I had soap, I couldn't get rid of the *mata gente*. It had gone too deep, to a place nothing could clean.

I tried to see my reflection in a small pool at the edge of the stream. But a breeze sent a series of ripples across the surface. My eyes looked crossed and my nose ran into my mouth. My face looked like a dozen different puzzle pieces. No matter which way I moved my head, the pieces wouldn't fit together. If I ever made it across *la línea*, I probably wouldn't even know myself.

After dark, I pushed my way through the cornfield until I came to the rocky railroad bed. I found a grassy spot off to the side and lay down. But sleep wouldn't come, so I sat up, my back against a stump, and stared out at the tracks. Every bad part of riding the *mata gente* came back to me. I didn't want to get back on the train. I hated the *mata gente*. But it was free, and it headed in the right direction. And I'd be alone, just like I was when I first started the trip. *Solo*. All alone.

I moved my hand slowly to Abuelita's medallion, out of habit now, to be sure it was still there. I made little circles with my right index finger on the smooth metal back. I made the circles again and again, nonstop, until I couldn't tell where my finger left off and the medallion began.

I dozed, off and on. Then, late, very late, I sensed something near. The train gangs again? Soldiers? Other migrants, like me? A dog or a wild cat? I didn't move, straining to hear. I got ready to run or hide. Something behind me rustled, ever so slightly. I turned, slowly.

There was Elena, peering out from the edge of the cornfield. Her black eyes shone, like a wild animal watching and waiting. The tears running down her face, reflected by the light of the full moon, gave her away.

Had she come to say good-bye? Had she come to say she was sorry? Was she thinking of coming with me after all? Did she finally realize that we'd be better off without Javi?

I didn't move. I was afraid I'd startle Elena, that she would bolt like a deer. I wanted one more chance to convince her I was right. I opened my mouth to speak, to just whisper, "Elena," to coax her closer. Before I could say it, Elena's face melted away and she was gone, without a sound. The night was still. If Elena was walking back through the corn, she was as quiet as a ghost.

Maybe I'd imagined her. Or maybe she really had come. I didn't know what was real anymore. Should I follow Elena? Should I go now, drag her back with me, make her get on the train? Would she do what I said, anyway?

Elena, my sister, *mi hermana*. Who knew what was the right thing to do? Sure, Javier might look after Elena, but what if something happened to him? He already looked exhausted, or sick. So what if I didn't know everything Javi knew. At least I was young and still strong. That had to count for something.

What was our best chance of making it? *Our* best chance, I said to myself again and again. I realized I no longer thought about it as *my* trip north. I couldn't stand the thought of Elena going north alone. I couldn't stand the thought of me going alone, either.

And maybe it didn't matter why I did it, but before the sun was up, I ran to the road as fast as I could. An old red truck belching black smoke was just pulling away.

"*¡Esperen!*" I waved my arms wildly above my head. "Wait for me!" Elena's head popped up from the bed of the truck. A large, joyful smile spread over her face.

"Stop!" she screamed. She banged with both fists on the rear window of the cab. "You have to stop! *¡Es* Miguel, *mi hermano!*"

The truck screeched to a halt. I ran to catch up and vaulted up over the back and into the truck bed. It was filled with burlap bags of coffee beans. The driver pointed to a large, bright blue tarpaulin.

"If we knock on the window, put this over you and hold still. We'll do our best, but if there's a checkpoint, and they decide to check . . . well." He didn't finish his sentence. There was only so much they could do. There was only so much we could expect.

For two days and nights, the truck lumbered noisily down rutted roads, highways, through *pueblitos*. We drove around the edges of the big cities, traveling through a countryside that turned increasingly dry and arid. Elena made me a nest out of the coffee-bean bags, with an extra one for a pillow. She made one for herself, right next to mine.

Once, the second day, Javi caught my eye. He nodded silently, as if to acknowledge something unsaid. It could've been a nod that said I'd made the right choice to not get back on the *mata gente*. Or maybe the nod was simply to say, "Okay, here we are again." I couldn't tell. Except for the nod, his face was blank.

I stared out at the land and kept my thoughts to myself. The only thing that mattered was making it across *la línea*. If the stories were true, the worst was yet to come. Once we crossed *la línea*, everything would change. Everything.

CHAPTER 24

The border town was dust. It poofed up around our feet as we walked. The hoods of cars, windowsills, a tattered blue awning above a closed shoe store, a single droopy mimosa tree next to the police station—everything was clothed in light brown.

Elena wiped her hand across the trunk of a parked taxi, then wrote *"Lávame"* with her index finger. Bright green paint showed through, glinting in the sun.

We walked toward the *mercado*, where my contact could be found. Elena and Javier walked side by side. Javi limped slightly, favoring his right ankle. With each step, he listed slightly toward Elena. She moved a little to the left, closing the gap between them.

We crossed the street and pushed our way onto the sidewalk on the other side. A crowd had gathered around the newsstand at the edge of the *mercado*. The headlines on three different newspapers screamed in giant letters:

¡Se Descarilla Tren!

¡Cientos Muertos!

¡El Mata Gente Mata a Muchos!

Javi grabbed a paper and held it so Elena and I could see. The *mata gente* had derailed at a high speed, hours north of where we had jumped off. Many were killed, maybe hundreds. Many more were injured, and most were children. The photos were big and scary. Little bodies lay scattered, like twigs, across a grassy slope.

"Was it *our mata gente*, Javi?" Elena asked.

"I don't know." Javi closed his eyes and took a deep breath. "It could've been. Or maybe the *mata gente* that came through the next day. Who knows?"

We read every word of every article in each of the papers, but they all said the same things. Equipment failure. A tragedy.

Children with no identification. A government investigation. Javi shook his head, as if the news confirmed what he'd already known. All I could think was that Elena and I had cheated death again. How much luck could we have left?

We threaded our way through the shoppers. "Don Clemente's instructions said to look for a guy in the boot stall, in the *mercado*," I explained.

There were the usual fruit and vegetable stalls. But there were others you'd find only at the border. One spot, El Coyote, sold supplies you needed to cross the desert: knives, snakebite kits, light jackets and pants, a dozen kinds of hats, and water bottles— hundreds and hundreds of blue and clear plastic water bottles.

People crowded around, pawing through the items. An older man in a cowboy hat cradled an armful of water bottles. Two teenage boys grabbed several pairs of pants with drawstrings.

"We need two pair each," one said to the other. "They said it gets cold at night. Get one bigger pair to layer, and to protect against scorpions."

A man and a woman in matching bright blue Windbreakers stood off to the side of El Coyote. The words "*Socorro Fronterizo*" were stitched onto the front of each jacket. They held thick stacks of pamphlets, handing one to every person who left the stall.

An older woman took the paper politely, folded it, and stowed it in her shirt pocket. "*Si Dios es servido, llegamos,*" she said. She thought it was all in God's hands. Nothing the pamphlet said would make a bit of difference to her.

Two young men about twenty years old each took one. They scanned the pamphlet briefly, shrugged their shoulders, and threw them to the ground as they walked off. Another looked at the paper quizzically. He frowned at the words but studied the drawings intently for several minutes.

"*Joven,*" the man said. He pressed a pamphlet into my hand. His touch was warm and firm. Kind eyes met mine. "Here. Take one. Read it."

"Guía de Seguridad en el Desierto." I glanced through the pages. Some of the advice was about desert safety, but most of it seemed to be about how to give yourself up, or how to get back to Mexico if you were lost.

> Tip #3: "If the Border Patrol intercepts you, keep
> your hands visible at all times.
> Never move them toward your pockets."
> Tip #7: "Follow the power lines south."

"But the best thing is, don't go," the man cautioned. "Go back home. It's very dangerous out there."

He spoke to me as if I were the only one he would talk to all day, as if I was his son or brother or best friend. He must talk to hundreds a day the same way he talked to me, but I bet he didn't convince more than one person a day to not try to cross.

"Gracias," I said. "We just need one. We're together."

I nodded toward Elena and Javi. A trail of warning pamphlets littered each of the pathways that led away from El Coyote, ground into the dirt by the heels of border crossers in a hurry. Elena took the pamphlet out of my hand and stuffed it in her front pocket.

At the far corner of the *mercado,* we found the one and only *botas* stall. The scent of new leather filled the air. Some boots sat displayed on shelves in the back. Others hung from the ceiling, out of reach. These were pointy-toed boots made of fine black, brown, tan, and white leather, with lots of tooling. These were boots for *misa,* for baptisms, for weddings, *quinceañeras*, and funerals.

A man sat in the middle of the stall on a short three-legged stool, hunched over a boot in his hands. He rubbed paste into the leather with his bare hands. He used a practiced, circular movement. With each pass, the leather became softer and more pliable. We watched the man silently for several moments.

He finally looked up, continuing to work the leather by touch.

He was not young, but his face was as smooth and unwrinkled as the leather he held. A carefully trimmed moustache covered his upper lip. His green eyes moved slowly from me to Elena to Javi.

"What can I show you?" he asked. "I have a fine pair right here. They would be perfect for you." He spoke to Javier first, out of respect, or practicality. Javi would be the one with money.

"We are looking for El Plomero," I replied quickly, cutting off Javier. I wanted to be the first to talk.

"I make boots. If you need a plumber, I know a good one." He bent once again to his work. I wondered if there was a code or a password or secret sign that Don Clemente forgot to tell me.

"No," I insisted, "I'm sure. He told me to ask for 'El Plomero' in the boot shop at the *mercado*. I'm sure that's what he said."

The man's head came up again. He raised one eyebrow ever so slightly. "Who told you?" he asked. He continued to soften the leather.

"Don Clemente told me," I said. "I was supposed to have been here days ago, but I was delayed."

"What's your name?" he demanded. "And what do you know about Don Clemente?" He stopped his work now. I had his full attention.

I didn't want to say much until I knew who this man was. I needed to know if he really was "El Plomero" or if he knew him. Most of all, I needed to know El Plomero's loyalty. Since Don Clemente's death, did he now work for Juanito? If he did, I couldn't trust him.

"My name is Miguel de Cervantes. Don Clemente arranged for El Plomero to help me." I didn't say the obvious—that El Plomero was to help me cross the border.

"I spoke to Don Clemente this morning." His eyes locked on mine. He didn't blink. "He said nothing about you," he continued. "Your name means nothing to me."

So he *was* El Plomero. That much was now clear. But what he said was a lie, and a test for me.

"Don Clemente is dead. He died in an accident. Juanito told me so himself," I answered.

And then I took a risk, to see if I could trust the man or not. The most I'd lose was this one *coyote*. There must be others, lots of others.

"Juanito either killed Don Clemente or had him killed," I declared. This thought had been forming in my mind for days, but it wasn't until I said it aloud that I knew it was the truth.

The man's eyes flickered. He stood up and placed the boots on the counter.

"You can tell that to your grandchildren, but for now, keep it to yourself," he warned. "Juanito is a worm, the lowest of the low. He's trying to take over. I worked for Don Clemente for over twenty years. I won't work for anyone else. And, yes, I am El Plomero."

He examined us again. "Is it the three of you, then, or just you?"

"The three of us . . . me, my sister, Elena . . . Javier . . ." I paused. "Originally, it was just me, but—"

El Plomero interrupted, "No matter. Be here at three. I'll have it all arranged."

CHAPTER 25

We returned to the boot stall at exactly three o'clock. Nothing so far had gone according to plan, but now with El Plomero, I allowed myself to feel a small bit of optimism. Maybe things would go the way Don Clemente had intended, finally.

The iron grill had been pulled down and locked up tight. Javi rattled the metal with both hands. Elena poked her nose through the grating and peered into the darkness. I pulled at both of the giant padlocks.

"Where is he?" Elena asked anxiously. "He said three. Do you think he's not coming?"

"Calm down, Elena," I replied. "He'll be here. He's probably just running late. We'll wait. At least it's cooler in here." It was a relief to escape the afternoon heat.

Javier sank down onto the concrete floor and leaned against the metal grill. He closed his eyes, pulled his ankle toward him, and rubbed it carefully. He probed the area above the anklebone, grimacing slightly.

Elena looked at him with concern. She sat down next to him, cross-legged, and motioned for him to prop up his ankle on her knee. Then she reached into her pocket and pulled out the pamphlet. She thumbed through the pages, scanning the contents.

"Listen to this," Elena said. "This is what happens if you don't drink enough water out in the desert."

I leaned over to check out "Danger Signs of Dehydration."

"Irritability. Angers easily," she read. "That's one of the first things to watch out for."

Elena gave me a little grin. "I finally know what's wrong with you! It looks like you've been dehydrated your whole life, Miguel."

I grabbed the pamphlet out of her hands and read the next

warning sign aloud. "Confusion. Makes irrational decisions."

"What? Is this whole thing about you?" I teased back.

Elena poked me in the ribs, and yanked the paper out of my hands. "Oh, yeah, well just look what it says next," she began.

"He's here," Javi interrupted. He was looking down the long corridor of stalls. Striding toward us, head high, was El Plomero.

"Come! We're running late," our *coyote* commanded.

He motioned for us to follow him. He unlocked the grating and pulled it up. As we stepped inside the boot stall, he quickly slammed the grating back down and locked it up tight. Then he moved to the back of the stall toward the shelves of boots and reached under the lowest shelf. I heard a small click, and a small section of the shelves swung out.

We walked through the opening, squeezing into the room behind the stall. The secret door closed. One dull bulb revealed a small storeroom stuffed from floor to ceiling with survival gear, organized by category.

"Here, try these." El Plomero shoved a pair of light but well-made synthetic hiking boots into my hands. I kicked off my worn-out sneakers and replaced my filthy, stinky socks with new, thick ones. The new boots fit perfectly. Elena tried on several pairs before she found ones she liked.

Javier selected a high-topped pair. He laced them, stood up, and took several tentative steps. He limped only a little. He nodded to himself and muttered, "These will do."

El Plomero gave us new pants, caps, and bandannas; two shirts to layer; and waterproof jackets, all in light colors. We each got a backpack stocked with raisins and packets of brown sugar, a small first-aid kit, and a tarpaulin. Mostly, though, the backpacks held as much water as we could carry.

El Plomero was a professional. He knew what he was doing. Nothing was left to chance. No wonder Don Clemente's fees were so high. No wonder they said he had never lost a single person.

"We leave now," El Plomero announced. "We have a full moon tonight. We need to take advantage of that."

I reached into my pocket and pulled out our remaining money. "Here. Take this. It's all we have left."

"We'll have plenty of time to take care of that later." El Plomero didn't touch the money. "I'm taking you myself. Don Clemente said I was to take special care of you. This is the last thing I'll do for him."

He looked at us hard. "It's at least two long nights of walking, perhaps more. It depends on your stamina, the weather, *la migra* . . . many, many things can happen in the desert. Most of them are unpleasant.

"We'll take a new route, to the west," El Plomero continued. "There's too much surveillance, too many other problems to the east. The new route is longer than the eastern one. It will be very difficult. If you're not able to withstand the heat and other hardships, you won't make it."

He paused, letting his words sink in. "I'm giving you one last opportunity to reconsider. You can turn around and go back home now."

Again he waited. Our silence filled up the little room. Did he really expect that we would back out? He didn't know what we'd come through. I wasn't about to give up yet. Elena was even more stubborn. And Javi? He'd never turn around. Never. This would be his only chance.

"You're like everyone else," El Plomero said matter-of-factly. His warnings had not changed our minds one bit. "Everyone believes they'll make it. And, of course, you must have faith, mustn't you? It's the only way to enter the wilderness."

He turned and opened a door that led to an alley outside. We piled ourselves and our gear into a dirty white pickup truck. Elena and El Plomero sat in front with the driver, Javi and I in the back.

For maybe an hour and a half, we headed west along a dirt

road. The driver swerved to avoid the worst of the potholes, but Javi and I flew up and down on the hard metal of the truck bed. The road gave way to a faint dirt track that ended abruptly at the edge of a dry gully.

We got out and stretched. The driver pulled plastic jugs from the toolbox in the truck bed and thrust them into our hands. We took long swigs of warm water, as much as we could, before the truck headed back to town. A large trail of dust marked its slow passage east. The sun had set, but the heat of the day still rose up from the sand under our feet.

We adjusted our bootlaces and backpack straps for comfort. My shoulders ached and we hadn't taken a single step. The water was heavy. Really, really heavy. I'd carried enough *agua* in San Jacinto, for the corn, to know that soon it would feel like I was hauling around a load of bricks.

Javi hefted his own pack higher on his shoulders and tightened the belt at the waist. I couldn't see that it made any difference. The weight just seemed to settle down low again, as if the water were pulling him toward the center of the earth. He grunted, tugged at the pack again, and cinched the shoulder straps even tighter. Sweat poured down his face, too much for the effort he was making.

El Plomero checked his own pack. He shifted some contents, reached into Elena's pack, took out three-quarters of her water and put it in his.

"I can carry it, Plomero," Elena insisted. "I want to do my share."

"No, you can't. You'll slow us down. We can't wait for you." El Plomero squared his shoulders.

"*Me llamo* Moisés," he added quietly. "You can call me Moisés."

With that, he faced north and began scrambling down the rocky slope into the gully. "*Vámonos,*" he commanded. "There's no time to waste. I set the pace."

He'd made his way across the wash and up the other side before we had even taken one step.

"Keep up. No one can afford to wait for anybody," Moisés's voice echoed across the emptiness. "We wait for no one."

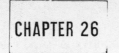

CHAPTER 26

The desert stretched out on all sides of us, flat and immense. We had unlimited space, but we walked single file behind Moisés, first Javi, then Elena, then me. Moisés hiked at a fast, steady pace. He stopped now and then to check his bearings. In the fading twilight, and then in the rising light of the moon, it was easy to see.

Perhaps two hours into the hike, we paused briefly. Moisés doled out raisins and a few almonds. Between bites, he gave us a lecture on basic survival.

"Unfortunately, this is the hottest time of the year. So don't talk more than you need to, even at night. It uses up moisture. Drink before you're thirsty. If you wait, it will be too late. Never take off any of your clothes. You lose water twice as fast if you're not covered up. We have just enough water to make it, if everything goes perfectly. Don't go anywhere without your pack. It has everything you need to survive, for a while anyway."

I didn't need to ask Moisés to repeat any of it. It's easy to learn something when it matters to you. Javi nodded, as if he already knew most of what Moisés said.

"Watch where you sit and where you walk, especially at night. Scorpions and rattlesnakes will be out, just like us," Moisés continued. "Don't sit on the ground, in the sun, during the day. Sit above the ground. Even a meter up, it may be ten to twenty degrees cooler. Take care of your feet. They're the only way to get out of here."

So, we had a whole new set of enemies here—the sun, the heat, the animals. We could stay for a short time only. If we stayed longer, we would pay with our lives.

"Of course, there's always *la migra* to worry about," Moisés said. "But here, in this section, once we cross the border, it's the militia we need to look out for. Ranchers have their own armies, equipped with uniforms and guns. And hatred for us."

Moisés turned his back to us and began to walk once again. He had long legs and took big steps. With my own height, I could match him stride for stride. Elena had to take almost two steps for every one of Moisés's. Javi was somewhere in between. Moisés didn't look back to see where we were. He kept up the same relentless pace. I fell into the rhythm of the hike.

I daydreamed about the end, the very end, my homecoming in California. Papá would hug me and not let go. He'd ask for my forgiveness. He'd say he'd made a big mistake by making me wait.

Mamá would cry and hold my hand and offer up small grateful prayers *a Dios*. Papá would crack open a beer and hand it to me and no one would say I was too young. They'd beg me to tell them everything.

Javi and Moisés, Colmillo, Capitán Morales—all would figure into the story, but I'd be the main character. I would, of course, give Elena some credit. And I'd have a big heart. I wouldn't blame Elena for any of the trouble she got us into. Elena would tell everyone how I saved us both.

I replayed this fantasy a hundred times in my mind. I was so deep into my thoughts that I didn't notice that I was now third in line. Moisés, Elena, then me. I looked back over my shoulder. Javier had fallen behind, way behind. He straightened up and walked evenly, just as I turned to look.

We stopped twice more, the second time just as pale gold and pink tinted the eastern horizon. It took Javi more than five minutes to catch up to us. Moisés frowned, checked the ground around us, and spread a tarpaulin for us to sit on. We drank the small rations of water that he allowed us. I wasn't hungry, but he insisted that we eat small portions of the energy bars.

"We move again in ten minutes," Moisés announced. "Two or three more hours, then we'll stop for the hottest part of the day.

Javier, come with me."

Moisés motioned for Javier to follow him. They moved out of hearing distance, but they needn't have bothered. We could guess what was being said. Moisés pointed at Javi's ankle. Javi shrugged, then raised his hands, palms up.

"Really," I could imagine him saying, "it's just a small sprain. It'll be fine again once we rest."

Then Moisés turned his back to us. He wanted to be sure we couldn't read his lips. But there were other things to read. I could hear the harsh tone of Moisés's words. I could see his stiff back, his shaking head.

It wasn't hard to understand what Moisés meant when his hands and fingers pointed first back toward Elena and me and then toward the rocky ground and the mountains that rose in the distance in front of us. The conversation might as well have been written out in the red sand at our feet or across the pale blue of the morning sky.

"He doesn't know Javi like we do, does he, Miguel?" Elena said. "Moisés doesn't know how strong Javi is."

I was silent. I didn't know if I should say what she wanted to hear or what I thought she needed to hear.

"¿*Qué piensas*, Miguel? I want to know what you think. Really, I do," Elena pleaded.

"Well, I think you're right," I replied. "Javi *is* strong. He's going to make it."

I couldn't see how telling the truth would help Elena make it out of this desert. She needed to believe that the three of us would survive together. Besides, what *was* the truth about Javi? He'd surprised me again and again with what he could do, with what he knew. He'd made it this far. Why not all the way?

Relief flooded her face. A single tear made its way down through the dirt on her cheek. "*Gracias*, Miguel. We can all make it, together. I just know it." She leaned over and kissed my cheek.

Javi and Moisés made their way back to us. Moisés kicked at the sand grimly, his eyes fixed on the ground. Javi had put on his best smile, but there was pain in his eyes.

"Hey, you two, guess what Moisés told me?" he said excitedly. "We're here! We're already here!"

I looked around, confused. "What do you mean? We're in the middle of the desert! We're not anywhere."

"No, no!" Javi said. "We *are* here. We crossed *la línea, la frontera* . . . sometime in the night."

Javi stretched out his arms as if to embrace the idea. "Don't you see? We made it! *¡Ya llegamos!*"

We all looked at the desolation that surrounded us. There was nothing but scrub brush and a single, tailless lizard skittering across the sand toward the safety of a rock.

I began to laugh first, then Elena and Javi. His big donkey laugh echoed across the desert. Moisés grinned. Soon we were laughing out loud. We laughed until our stomachs hurt and we couldn't laugh anymore.

I laughed so hard that I cried. It was crazy . . . *una tontería*. I'd arrived at the very place I always wanted to be, across *la línea* in *el Norte*, but I was in the middle of nowhere.

Had I come this far to feel just like I did in San Jacinto? To be somewhere and nowhere at the same time? To belong and be lost at the same time?

We fell silent. The tension had lifted. Elena sighed, almost contentedly. Moisés set himself to the task of charting our course; Javi stood next to him, closely studying the landmarks that Moisés pointed out.

"I always thought I'd know exactly the moment I crossed the border," I admitted, folding up the tarpaulin. "I thought I'd feel it, somehow. But I didn't even know. I had no idea. How could I not have felt something?"

Moisés, who had most likely crossed the border dozens of

times, just shrugged. And with that, he strode off toward the North at an even faster pace than before.

CHAPTER 27

The morning started out cool, but the reprieve from the heat didn't last long. Moisés led us northeast across the sandy desert floor. Javi still brought up the rear, and Elena had also now fallen behind me. She didn't complain or ask to stop once, even though the sun now beat down relentlessly. And then the terrain turned uneven and rocky, but it didn't slow Moisés down one bit.

We stopped before noon at a large outcropping. It consisted of several large boulders leaning against each other at odd angles.

"We stop here for the afternoon." Moisés motioned us to the eastern side of the rocks.

"The rocks will give us some shade during the hottest part of the day. The shadows will get longer later in the afternoon," he explained.

In the shade, Moisés rationed out several large gulps of water and packets of brown sugar.

"Get out the tarps." He reached into his own backpack. "Once I check for rattlers, we'll spread them out and rest."

He cautiously inspected several likely spots for snakes: underneath a ledge jutting out from one of the rocks, an indentation between two of the boulders, and a hole that appeared to lead down into the ground right next to where our heads would be when we stretched out.

"Good," he announced. For the first time, he smiled. He was clearly in charge, in his element. "We've made decent progress. We're just where we should be."

He kicked a few random rocks out of the way. His smile widened. "We were lucky to get such a nice hotel this time of year. People just can't seem to get enough of this place. They're dying to come here!"

Moisés pointed to the left. "Your room is here, Javier. Sorry, Miguel and Elena, you'll have to share a suite."

"That's okay," I replied. "We're used to it." If Moisés felt like we could have a little fun, I'd play along.

I pictured the postcards of the fancy Acapulco hotel Tío had worked at, before he got lonely for Tía and the kids and came back home. All I could remember was the water, pool after pool of perfect, clear blue water.

"I think I'll go down to the pool later for a swim. Anyone want to go with me?"

"I'll go," Elena chimed in. "But first I'm going to take a nap in this nice, big, soft bed." She patted the hard ground under the tarp.

"For me, a hot shower, first. Then, a steak, *papas fritas*. Maybe two steaks." Javi smacked his lips.

"Well, enjoy your stay," Moisés said. "I'll wake you when it's time to check out."

He lay down flat on his back on the far edge, closed his eyes, and appeared to be asleep within moments. He probably made the same joke every time he came through here with a group of *pollitos*. Things were going well. We all felt like we could afford a joke.

Elena picked up the corner of the tarp nearest her and checked for rattlers one last time. She seemed satisfied and rolled over onto her side. Javi loosened his boots slightly but didn't take them off. He sighed, lay back, put up one knee, and propped his bad ankle on top.

I lay for some minutes just listening, but all I heard was our own breathing. I thought I heard the roar of a small engine far, far off, but the sound was gone before I was sure I'd heard it. A hawk screeched after prey. A whiff of a hot breeze blew silently across the sand, just enough to move a few grains here and there. The sand moaned softly, then went quiet again.

I filled up the silence with imagining the sound of Abuelita's voice, gravelly and low, talking and humming to herself as she worked. What would she say if she saw this place? I bet she and Doña Maria would say to beware. I fell asleep holding Abuelita's medallion in my right hand.

I woke to Moisés's voice, low and urgent. "I heard something. I'm going to investigate. Stay here. Don't move. I'll be back quickly."

Moisés picked up his pack and headed around the northern edge of our outcropping. Elena hunkered down next to the closest boulder. Javi and I crawled as far as we could in the shelter of the stones. Then we crouched and peered out around the last rock.

Moisés was making his way north across a stretch of rolling dunes. Beyond the dunes were several small hills dotted with cactus. He went up and down with the landscape, finally disappearing beyond the crest of the first hill.

"It's probably nothing," Javi said knowingly. "The desert can play tricks on you. It can make you believe things are there that aren't.

"You know about a mirage, the trick of light," he continued. "Distances, too, they trick you. Things look closer than they really are. The illusions are everywhere."

He crawled back to Elena. They both took drinks from Javi's water supply. My mouth was bone dry and fuzzy, so I checked my own water. Almost half of it was gone. Moisés had done a good job of rationing. I drank thirstily. The rocks cast giant shadows now. I figured we'd been out for twenty-four hours. *Muy bien.* We'd make it. Moisés had led us into this place, and he would lead us out.

And then, the *crack!* of a rifle echoed across the desert from the north. Elena's head jerked up. Javi froze. No more shots followed the first, but fear spread through my arms and legs. I didn't feel the heat anymore. I was colder than I'd ever been.

"It could be *la migra*. They could've fired a warning shot, perhaps," said Javi. "But I don't think it's the law. It's the other ones, the militia that Moisés said would be here." He bent quickly to fold up the tarps and stow the remaining water.

Elena didn't budge, except for her head. It moved side to side, like radar scanning for signs of life. "Shh!" she said. "Did you hear that? I heard something else!"

No one moved. From the north came the whine of an engine straining to mount a hill. I crawled once more to the edge of the outcropping to search for any sign of Moisés. Coming down the closest hill and across the dunes was an open four-wheel-drive vehicle. An oversized United States flag flew from the antenna.

Two men in military-type camouflage fatigues sat in front. The one in the passenger seat held his rifle ready, the sun reflecting off his wraparound sunglasses. Moisés's long body lolled across the backseat.

They appeared to be heading straight toward us. I crouched lower. "Don't move!" I turned to warn Javi and Elena. "Keep down! It's the militia!"

Not more than one hundred meters from us, the driver turned the vehicle toward the west. Moisés's head rolled to one side, his eyes closed. He held one hand to his right shoulder where blood oozed from a wound. Cradled in his other arm was his backpack.

I started to get up, but Javi pulled me back. The last thing I saw was Moisés slowly pushing his backpack out of the side of the jeep. It landed with a soft thud on the desert floor.

Javi, Elena, and I sat, unmoving, for many minutes. We waited until we could no longer hear the sound of the engine, until silence descended again on the desert. We stood together and looked to the west. There was no sign of the jeep, not even a hint of dust.

"He threw his backpack out as close as he could to us. It's over there." I pointed to the black blob in front of us.

We approached the pack slowly, as if it were alive, and dangerous. A dark circle of wetness spread out around it.

"*Es mi agua*," Elena said, pointing at the wet sand. "He had the rest of my water."

She knelt down, picked up the pack and turned it over easily.

The bullet in Moisés's shoulder had first ripped through both sides of the pack, leaving a hole big enough to put your finger through.

Elena pulled her hands away from the pack. They were rosy pink, a mixture of Moisés's blood and the water he was carrying, the same colors as the sunset on the western horizon.

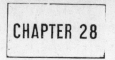

CHAPTER 28

It was just the three of us again. I'd started out my journey alone. Elena had made us become two, then Javi had made us become three. Moisés made four. We should have finished as four. I didn't like the math.

Moisés was gone. Everything he knew about the desert, good and bad, was gone. His water and most of Elena's was all gone, swallowed by the desert sand. I had less than half of my water, Javi about the same. Water couldn't be stretched. Even with the best of luck, there was enough for two of us, not three. More math.

We were going to make it, or we weren't. We were going to live, or we were going to die. So, right off, we broke two of the rules Moises had spelled out for us. First, we sat right on the ground. Second, we talked, more than we had to. Behind the boulders, we made a plan.

"We'll walk again tonight, as far as we can," Javi said. "Moisés said to head to the east of that mountain."

He pointed at the jagged peak that loomed in the distance to the north. One kilometer away? Ten? Twenty? More?

"There, somewhere, is a town, and a highway. West for you two. East for me."

Javi held out his thumb, as if he were hitching a ride. In Moisés's pack we'd found some twenty-dollar bills. It seemed like enough to buy us bus tickets or a ride, but who knew?

I didn't have much experience with dollars. Papá and Mamá could never get enough dollars together to send for us, even when they worked nonstop, day and night. Maybe one of those twenty-dollar bills was like nothing in California. Maybe people carried around dozens of them, big piles of them, just to buy a bit of goat meat or some milk or to put a little gas in the car.

Javi looked to the east. "How far do you think we can see? How far before there's a river or a stream, any water at all?"

I shrugged. There was nothing to block our view. The sky had turned from dark blue to a blue so deep it was nearly black. There was no hint of the horizon, no clue as to where the desert, or the earth, ended.

"New York is over there, somewhere. If I just walk east, I'll get there. I'll see my brother. He's waiting for me, you know. He's expecting me, soon. All I have to do is get there."

Javi stood up and took a few steps eastward. He seemed ready to take off into the darkness at that moment, in the wrong direction.

"Javi." I rose to stop him.

"You take the lead," Javi said, turning back to me. "Walk at Moisés's pace. I'll keep up. Don't worry about me. You have to make it tonight . . . you don't have a choice."

"What if we don't make it?" Elena asked quietly. "What if we get lost, or we run out of water?"

"We're going to make it, Elena." I said it as much for my benefit as for hers. I let the possibility of failure creep up from deep in my mind, then pushed the thought back down. Failing now meant dying. "It's too late to give up now, isn't it?"

"But what if *one* of us can't make it?" Elena persisted. She wanted everything spelled out.

Even in the heat, goose bumps popped up on my arms. Goose bumps, not for a *chupacabra* or *La Llorona* or stolen body parts. They were a result of cold, deep fear at having to make a choice that no one should have to make. *Escalofríos, no de fantasmas, sino de vida y muerte.*

"It's all of us or none of us," Elena declared. "We won't leave anyone behind. We won't . . . I won't. I can't."

"It won't come to that. It doesn't have to come to that. If worse comes to worst, give yourselves up to *la migra.*" Javi grabbed the edge of a boulder to steady himself. His breath came again in ragged puffs.

"Look," he pointed out matter-of-factly. "It's better to be alive to try again. You're young. Your whole life is in front of you. If you cross enough times, you'll make it sooner or later."

So we set out. Before the moon rose, the night was as black as black could be. I tried to walk quickly but I had to watch every step to avoid a rock or a rut or a cactus in our way. Then, when the moon did rise, we came to terrain crisscrossed with ravines. We slid down the soft earth and sand on one side, picked our way across, and climbed clumsily up the other side.

Javi and Elena grunted behind me as we crossed through our third ravine. The bottom of it was covered with stunted mesquite and chaparral. We had to push our way through thorny branches that punctured our arms, even through our long sleeves. Deep scratches soon covered my palms and the backs of my hands. Was this the route that Moisés intended to take? Maybe he knew a different path around this part of hell.

But we didn't stop. After midnight, clouds began to cover the moon. I paused briefly to check our progress. The mountain was still in the right position, but it didn't look much closer than before. I was disheartened, but I kept it to myself.

More clouds built up across the sky and, to the east, a mighty bolt of lightning cut down to the ground. Thunder followed. I sniffed the air. The smell of newly wet earth reached us. It was raining to the east.

Huge sheets of lightning showed our way briefly, followed by deafening thunder and then complete darkness. We had to stop to let our eyes adjust to the change. Each time, the lightning seemed more blinding. Each time, the darkness seemed darker. The thunder reverberated in my skull and my ribs and my shins.

Then, suddenly, it started to rain. It was a hard, pounding downpour that soaked us within seconds, before we even had a chance to pull out our jackets. We stood and let the water stream over us for several minutes. The storm passed as quickly as it came.

It lasted long enough to cool the temperature by maybe thirty degrees. It didn't last long enough for water to collect, water we needed, badly.

"Now what?" Elena asked me, her teeth chattering wildly.

"Change. We take off the wet shirts and put on our jackets. We'll dry the shirts tomorrow." I was making this up as I went along. It seemed like a good thing to do, or the only thing we could do.

So we changed. And we walked, and we walked, and we walked. The ground leveled to a sort of valley. I thought I found a faint trail. It was narrow, but it headed in the right direction. I lengthened my stride, hoping to make up for time we'd lost earlier in the night. I moved to avoid a branch on my left, brushing up against a cactus on the right.

"Ow!" I complained. I rubbed my hand, and the pain intensified. Hundreds of tiny spurs covered my fingers. I bent to see if I could pick them out, but the light was too dim. There were too many anyway.

"Ah, these are the *chollas* I heard of." Javi took out his comb and handed it to me. "They penetrate your skin and stick in. Rake them off. It's the only way."

A *cholla* had also attacked Elena. She sniffled in pain but said nothing. We took turns with Javi's comb many times that night. Every stop cost us precious time and energy.

What was this place trying so hard to protect? Why bother with fences or *la migra* or militias? The heat, the cold, the snakes, the evil *cholla* spurs—they all conspired to keep us out or slow us down or outright kill us.

I tried and tried, but I couldn't seem to find a route straight toward our landmark. Whenever I headed us north, a ravine or cactus or part of a barbed-wire fence made us veer either east or west. Each time, it slowed us down. Twice we ducked down flat and hid when headlights flickered on a dirt road. We believed it was *la migra* out on patrol.

But I worried most about something else. We were going slowly, yet Javi continued to fall behind. He caught up when we stopped, but each time it took him longer to reach us. The rough terrain had to be hurting his ankle. At dawn, I turned to watch Javi struggle toward us yet again. He limped slightly, but it was more than that. He looked shrunken and wizened, as if the desert were sucking out his insides.

Elena came up right next to me. She squinted her eyes toward the mountain. It now appeared to be several kilometers away. "It looks closer. How much farther, do you think?"

I remembered what Javi said about illusions in the desert. I had no idea how far we had to go. I looked at her, then at me. Our condition was the opposite of illusion. Deep scratches covered our hands, arms, faces. Barbed wire had torn my shirt in front and one knee of my pants. One thorn was deeply embedded in my forearm. It would be infected soon if I didn't get it out. Elena's face was badly sunburned. She sat and pulled off her left boot. A blister, broken and leaking fluid, covered her heel.

But the worst part of it all was the thirst. I'd allowed us only small sips of water during the night. But what was it that Moisés said? Something about not getting too thirsty. Something about not saving the water. I couldn't make sense of that advice. I figured we had enough left for a small amount each. Then it would be gone anyway.

It was early morning and already the sun had no mercy. I didn't want to think about how hot it was going to get. I pulled out the water and swallowed several small drinks. Elena watched me closely and then took exactly the same amount for herself. Javi barely wet his lips.

"Drink," Elena and I said together. He put the bottle up to his lips and rolled his head back.

"Listen, you two," Javi said slowly, stowing his water bottle in his pack. "I have something to tell you." His usual fast talk had slowed to a crawl. His words slurred together. Everything about him seemed to have slowed down.

"Miguel is in charge now." He looked at Elena to make his point. "Do what he says."

Then he seemed to summon something from deep within. He pushed himself up, groaning with each movement. "You'll make it. I promised, remember? And I'll be right behind you, every step of the way."

CHAPTER 29

The sun beat down fiercely and the heat rose up from the ground in wavy, pulsating bands. Once, mid-morning, Javi stopped suddenly. He let his pack slide to the sand and began to fumble with the buttons on his long-sleeved shirt.

"It's hot," he mumbled to himself. "I'll be cooler."

"No, Javi!" I pulled his hands away from his chest. "Remember what Moisés said?"

Javi wrinkled his brow. "Moisés?" he asked. "Moisés? Oh, yes, him." But he gave me a puzzled look as I heaved his pack up and placed the straps around his shoulders.

I forced us to go on an hour more, but it was clear we needed rest, Javi more than anyone. The best protection I could find was a scrawny stand of mesquite bushes. They gave poor shade, but it was better than nothing, maybe.

We spread our tarps the way Moisés showed us. I looked around for snakes. Elena looked farther and harder, but even she gave up after a minute or two. A snake seemed like a small thing, or just another thing. It seemed neutral, a part of this place. I didn't have enough energy to care about a *culebra*.

I slept off and on. We moved to try to stay in the shade, but more than half of my body stayed out in the sun. I tried to lick my lips but I couldn't find enough saliva to do it. A steady wind came up that seemed to suck the last bit of water out of my body.

Late in the afternoon, I watched a dusty brown scorpion climb up my shirt sleeve to my chest, just below my chin. It stopped, as if it might stay. It held its tail high, at the ready. I took in a breath, very slowly, held it, and waited.

But the scorpion suddenly scurried away, down my body, and disappeared on the other side of the mesquite. Was the scorpion another omen? I decided that once we finished the water, we'd have to give ourselves up to the first person we saw. We'd die otherwise.

The sunset was a hundred different colors, but the sun itself was a blurry blob. The wind flapped our tarps as we folded them up for the last time. It picked up the sand in miniature tornados and sent them dancing across the desert. I led us north . . . again . . . the wind now blowing at a steady pace from the west.

"Look!" Elena pointed toward the sun. It dipped low on the horizon, completely hidden by a red-brown haze.

"Why does it look so strange?" she asked. "That's not a cloud. What is it?"

"I'm not sure," I replied. "But the weather is changing again. Can't you feel it?"

Elena paused, took her bandanna and wrapped it around her face to cover her nose and mouth as protection against the stinging sand.

I kept myself going by telling myself that this was the last stretch. Just one more step, Miguel. Don't stop, Miguel. *No te des por vencido,* Miguel. *Amáchate,* Miguel. If you stop, Elena and Javi will stop, too. *No pares*, Miguel.

We climbed up and down a series of small hills dotted with cactus. The hot wind pushed us to the side, like a mighty hand. On the far side of the first hill, a red toothbrush poked out of the desert floor, bristles first. I bent and picked it up. It was light, almost weightless, really.

I turned the toothbrush over and over. Who dropped it here? Was this the first thing abandoned? Was it the very last thing given up?

Then I made another decision. Not only would we leave no person in the desert, but we would leave no thing in the desert. If we left even one thing, it would mean we'd given up. I saw now that it was my job to not let us give up.

Twenty or thirty steps later, Elena found a plastic water bottle like ours. The blowing sand had already covered part of it. She examined the whole surface, as if she half expected to see the name of the owner marked somewhere on the plastic.

Another bottle leaned crookedly against a cactus, its top gone. A pair of child's sneakers, tied together by the laces, straddled the base of the plant. The soles of the shoes had melted in the heat. A torn blue work shirt hung from one of the arms of the cactus. The wind picked up the shirt and sent it flying to the east, along with the blowing sand, its arms extended ghostlike in the dusk.

On the far side of the next small hill, I spotted a shape lying next to a large, smooth rock. Even in the fading light, I could tell it was human. I stopped, waiting for Elena and Javi to come up next to me. Javi's cheeks had hollowed. His lips were scabbed over, his eyes dull and flat. He stared ahead at the blob in front of us.

"Stay here," I told Elena and Javi. "Let me look."

I approached slowly. It was a woman. She lay on her side, curled up. Her long black hair fanned out from her head. The skin on her face had blistered and puckered up. I couldn't tell how old she might be. Cradled in her arms was a small child, its face turned toward her breast.

Javi and Elena were beside me. Javi fell to the sand. He crossed himself. Then he crawled on his knees, a penitent at a shrine, three slow steps toward the bodies.

"Eduardo . . . *m'ijo* . . . Magdalena, *m'ija*," he muttered.

Elena inched closer to my side, grabbed my hand, and squeezed. She furrowed her brow in concern. Javi had confused the bodies with his own children.

"Dios los guarde. . . ." The wind muffled the rest of Javi's words.

"We can't just leave them, Miguel." Elena's grip tightened. "We should bury them."

"No." I pointed to the mother's feet, already covered with sand. The desert would take care of the burial. "We need to save our energy."

Who was she? Where did she come from? Where was she going? Who would wait for her, and the child, only to have them never appear? The desert had claimed her life and the life of her child. It would now take them away completely.

I took Javi's elbow to help him up. He pushed me away, continuing to pray in a barely audible whisper. Twice more, I tried to lift him to his feet. Finally, he allowed Elena to take his hand and pull him up.

We walked now side by side, the three of us, at Javi's pace, very slowly. We'd lose each other if we weren't close. The wind began to blow violently. In the driving sand, I couldn't see the mountain. I couldn't even see my fingers when I stretched out my arms in front of me.

If we didn't go on, we would run out of water and time. If we did go on, we'd run the risk of walking in circles or back, in the wrong direction. But we were in the middle of a giant desert sandstorm, and there were no good choices.

"We have to stop!" I yelled over the wind to Elena and Javi. "Get out the tarps! We'll curl up in them and wait this thing out. Maybe it won't last long, and we can go on."

We took off our backpacks, dug into them, and pulled out the tarps. Our water bottles were nearly empty. I shared the rest of mine with Elena. There didn't seem to be any point anymore in saving the water. Javi had already curled up inside his tarp like a butterfly in a cocoon, his backpack tucked close to his chest.

"*Tengo miedo,* Miguel." Elena's voice wavered weakly. "I don't want to be alone."

We strained against the driving sand to make our own cocoon, one tarp under us, the other tucked in as tight as we could make it around our bodies. By then the wind was howling fiercely.

We lay side by side. In the muffled darkness, the screaming wind all around us, I could barely make out her words.

"Are you mad at Papá, Miguel? I'm not mad at Mamá. Don't be

mad, Miguel," Elena murmured. She felt for my hand and intertwined her fingers with mine.

"It'll be better in California than we ever dreamed, right, Miguel? It'll be worth the wait, won't it?" She held tightly for a moment, then loosened her grip. She was too tired to hold on hard.

"You let me come with you. You didn't send me back to San Jacinto, like I deserved. *No me abandonaste,*" she whispered. "*Gracias,* Miguel. *Gracias.*"

Darkness fell. The storm got worse with each minute. Despite our efforts to block out the sand, it crept into our shelter. We kept our bandannas over our noses and mouths to filter it out, but I could still feel the grit between my teeth.

Elena slept beside me, exhausted. But I lay awake, listening to the wind. It was a thousand voices competing to be heard. Hundreds moaned in despair, hundreds in sadness. It was the people lost in this place, calling me to join them. It was the mother and child we left, now arisen and walking with the others.

It was *La Llorona* out to bewitch me, just as Doña Maria had warned. If I listened and followed, I'd be lost forever. With the last little piece of resistance I had, I plugged my ears with my fingers to shut out the sounds. And, finally, somehow, I slept.

CHAPTER 30

I put my head under the waterfall, tilted it back, and took big deep drinks of cold water. Lalo pulled me into the pool, wrestling me down into the green depths. Our arms and legs tangled and we burst to the surface, laughing and gasping for air.

Chuy reached into his pocket for his carving—bright green horns, red claws, blue fangs, yellow-spotted wings—and put it in my hand. The creature fit easily on my palm. I touched its head, between the horns. It turned and looked at me, then jumped spryly to the ground.

It grew, in an instant, bigger than a horse. "Get on!" Chuy and Lalo shouted together. They dived into the pool and came up as one. Their heads were bobbing black balls on the water.

"Chuy! Lalo!" I cried as the creature lifted me off the earth. "¡Adiós!"

They didn't turn around. Maybe they couldn't hear me. Or maybe they'd forgotten me already.

The creature circled higher and higher into the sky. Abuelita's rancho was a tiny little speck in the patchwork of green-brown fields. Up, up, we went. Then we headed south.

"North!" I commanded. But the creature didn't obey. It flew south, to Guatemala and the river. It gleamed below us and, from thousands of feet up, I was able to see every rock, every tree branch, each obstacle in the river's path.

The creature dived down sharply. Desperately, I tightened my hold on the horns. We swooped low over the water, and I saw it wasn't water at all, but a giant wall of sand.

I felt my grip slipping, and then I fell, slowly, slowly, deeper and deeper into the very middle of the mass.

I woke to a suffocating weight on my chest and legs, complete darkness and stillness. I was dead, or this was what it felt like to be buried alive. My heart beat faster and harder, as if it would burst out of my chest. I tried to scream, but no sound came out of my mouth.

"Miguel! Miguel!" Elena pulled my bandanna off my face. "Help! I think we're covered in sand!"

Her movements caused the weight on me to shift slightly. It was just enough to loosen up my fear so I could move. I pushed with all my strength on the tarp and Elena did the same.

We broke out of our cocoon to a world swept clean by the sandstorm. The mountain, our landmark, loomed to the left of us. By luck, by chance, by the grace of God, we had ended up where we needed to be. The sky was a brilliant blue and, for once, the morning was cooler. If we'd had water, I could even have felt happy.

"Javi," Elena whispered next to me. "*¿Dónde está* Javi?"

"What do you mean?" I asked. "He's there, asleep." I pointed to his tarp and the lump under it.

"No." Elena's voice was flat. "No, that's not Javi. It's not big enough. It's not him."

I picked up his tarp. The only thing inside the green cloth was Javi's backpack. Elena dropped her eyes, unzipped the pack, and pulled out what we expected to find.

There was Javi's water bottle. The last of the liquid sloshed in the bottom third of the bottle. It was most of the water that Javi was supposed to drink the day and night before. Except for small sips, he'd stopped drinking his water.

I took the bottle. There might be enough left to get Elena and me to someone who could help us. I didn't care if it was *la migra*, even the militia. Elena's face had sunk now, too. We didn't have much time left.

"We can find him, Elena. He can't have gone far, not in his condition." I turned around and around, scanning the desert in every direction.

"No," Elena answered. "No, Miguel. He wanted to go."

What was she saying? My own thinking was slow. I knew Javi's water was here and he was gone, but I couldn't somehow put the two together in a way that made sense.

"Besides, maybe he made it already," she continued.

Her voice sounded like Javi's had before the dust storm. Her words slurred and ran together. "He could've, you know, if he went in the right direction . . . if it wasn't too far. . . ."

Elena began to cry, quietly. How did her body find enough water to make tears? They traveled in small tracks down her blistered and swollen face. They mixed with the dust to form little muddy rivers of sorrow.

Maybe Javi had gotten so dehydrated that he didn't know what he was doing. Maybe he took off in the middle of the sandstorm, sure that New York was just over the next hill. Or maybe he'd crawled off, like a sick or injured animal would, to die alone.

But I wanted to believe Elena was right. Javi left with a purpose, and left his water behind with a purpose. He knew his footsteps would be covered by the wind-driven sand long before we woke. He knew we wouldn't be able to follow him. There was no way of knowing where he went or how far he might have gone. He knew Elena and I would have no choice but to go on together, just the two of us, alone, without him.

I took Javi's water, drank a few small sips, and handed the rest to Elena. She tilted the bottle to her cracked, swollen lips. I held it up for her, until every last drop had trickled down, out of the sparkling blue plastic, into her waiting mouth.

We packed everything up, even Javi's pack and tarp, and walked north. The crystal-clear day soon gave way to clouds, at first fluffy white and billowing. To pass the time, to forget our pain, Elena and I played an old childhood game, naming the shapes we saw in the clouds: a pirate ship, a two-headed goat, the engine of the *mata gente*.

And then, fantasies of the food we would eat: three scoops of strawberry ice cream, a giant *limonada, cinco enchiladas, carne asada, arroz, frijoles,* watermelon, and glass after glass after glass of ice-cold water.

And we never stopped looking, either one of us, for a sign of Javi. Our eyes moved over the landscape, searching for any unusual shape or movement. At regular intervals, we even turned around and scanned the desert we'd left behind us.

In the sky, a hawk circled. On the ground, a desert hare bounded for its hole. Army ants scavenged. A tortoise crawled, unconcerned, across a wide expanse of flat rock. But that was all. That was all we saw.

Then black clouds came on the wind, clouds promising rain. I shivered, remembering the storm from before. But the wind was as thirsty as we were. It pulled the rain skyward before it could reach the ground. Silvery trails of water descended from the clouds, then disappeared, phantomlike, into the air. It rained and rained, high in the sky, yet not one drop of water hit the bone-dry earth.

A bolt of lightning appeared to strike the earth some kilometers in front of us and then, several seconds later, the thunder rolled toward us. A low hum reached my ears. Was it the thunder echoing from far off? The drone continued, a steady roar of sound. I imagined it to be water, or millions of people, the mighty rushing river of my dream.

Elena's eyes were half-closed. She took smaller and smaller steps. She mumbled a conversation with Abuelita, as if she were right in front of us, nonsense about going to find Javi. Soon Elena wouldn't be able to walk or talk or think at all. Neither would I.

I pulled her by her fingertips, ever so slowly, to the top of the last hill. Elena sank to the ground in a heap, unable to move. I fell beside her, and raised my eyes to the sound rushing toward us.

There, below us, a steady stream of traffic sped east and west on a big multilane highway. The road ran just where Moisés said it would, right beyond the mountain. It slashed across the desert as if the vastness were nothing. I concentrated on the traffic heading west toward California. The sun reflected off car rearview mirrors, trailer taillights, and the windows of giant semis. Quick bursts of light, impossibly radiant, blinded me with their brilliance.

THE PHONE CALL

If I crane my neck, I can just barely see the bridge out of one corner of the window in my small third-floor apartment. The morning rays bounce off the bright blue of the bay and the dark orange of the span. The fog begins to move in toward the city, a white, wispy mass that will soon obscure the sun, the bay, the bridge. The day will be gray and chilly and windy. It's summer, and I'll wear my thick black sweatshirt later.

I return to my little desk, pick up my cup of *café con canela*, and take a sip. Laid out in front of me are two photos. In both, the sun shines brilliantly. If I close my eyes, I can almost remember the warmth. Beside the photos is Abuelita's *Virgen de Guadalupe* medallion.

I pick up my phone and punch in the numbers. It rings, distantly, just once.

"*Hola*, Miguel," Elena says before I speak. She's expecting my call.

"I got the picture. I still can't believe you graduated from college, and with a degree in English, of all things," Elena begins. We always talk about the California pictures first, the ones I send her. San Jacinto comes second.

"Mamá looks good, but Papá looks old, Miguel."

"I know, Elena. I know." I look at my copy of the picture, now framed, on the wall.

Papá's hair is white now, and some of his *canas verdes* are my fault. I made him suffer for the black emptiness I felt on the *mata gente*. It took me years to accept that Papá did what he did out of love, not pride.

Papá refused to be obligated to Don Clemente—a complicated and dangerous man—in any way. He rebuffed every one of Don

Clemente's offers to help, until he could no longer stand it. Then, finally, no *línea* mattered.

"What do you think of the twins?" I ask.

"They look so grown up! I can't wait to see them next summer when they come to visit."

I've grown to love my little sisters, the *hermanas* I'd never known or held until I came north. The *cuates* are smart, a little sassy, and strong, like Elena. But I feel a familiar twinge of envy. Maria and Liliana have advantages they don't appreciate or understand. Papá and Mamá made sure their Spanish is good, but English might as well be their first and only language, the way the words just tumble out of their mouths so naturally and easily.

Papá and Mamá never left my sisters' sides, not even for a day. Maria and Liliana never had to wonder when, or if, they would see their parents again. And the twins are citizens. They can go to Mexico and come back whenever they want. For them, there is no *línea.*

"What do you think of *my* pictures?" Elena asks.

I take my time. I don't want to hurry with this call, this one we make once a year, on this day.

I pick up the first photo. There's Elena, the one who claimed she wanted to go north more than anyone, right back there on Abuelita's *rancho* in San Jacinto. Elena returned as soon as Papá let her, right after she finished high school. Even Mamá wasn't enough to keep her in California. She says that *el Norte* never measured up to what she imagined it would be.

Elena is standing amidst her tomatoes, organic ones, in yellow, orange, red, even pink. In her hands she holds a chunk of organic goat cheese, whatever that is. She brags that her foods are becoming very popular in *la capital,* at the best restaurants.

"What's up with your hair?" I ask. "Are you growing it out, or what?" Gone is her little cap of short black hair. It's longer, falling now to her chin, framing her face in gentle waves of black.

"It's been ten years, Miguel," she announces. "It's time to move on."

I don't remind her that she said she'd never grow it out. She vowed to keep it short, the way Javi cut it before the *mata gente*, to help her remember *los sacrificios* people make for each other.

"I can't ever forget Javi, anyway. It doesn't matter what my hair looks like," she says. "You think about him, too. I know you do."

She can still read my mind. And I can still read hers. Elena wants to believe that Javier might have made it out of the desert, somehow. Javi could have survived, somehow. He could be working in New York, just like he said. He could have sent for his family, and they're all together. I don't think so.

"Miguelito is big, isn't he?" Elena says.

There, in the next picture is Chuy, holding *mi sobrino*. Chuy's smile spreads all the way across his wide face, a picture of pure happiness. He had to beg and beg, but Elena finally agreed to marry him. The baby was born a year ago. He is named Miguel Javier Moisés. Elena chose his names, and the sequence. She says it is the correct order.

"Good thing he looks like Chuy," I tease.

"*Cállate, feo,*" Elena says back. "Good thing he doesn't look like his *tío*. Guess what? There's a catalog in the States that might be interested in some of Chuy's and the others' artwork. Say a prayer. We could make some money, maybe, for a change."

"It's about time," I say. I pause.

"And the package, Miguel?" Elena asks finally. I was wondering how long it would take her to get around to it. "You were supposed to send Abuelita's medallion. Why didn't you?"

I gather my thoughts. Elena waits. And we both remember.

Ten years ago, to the day, Elena and I left San Jacinto. Nine years ago, to the day, Abuelita died. Her heart failed her. Doña Maria found her sitting in a chair in the kitchen, a pile of *chiles* in front of her ready to be peeled, the kind that bring fierce tears if their juices touch your fingers, and then your eyes. She is buried at the edge of the old cornfield on her beloved *rancho*.

"I still have the medallion," I finally confess. "I know we agreed that this year she'd be reunited with *la Virgen,* but—"

"But today's the anniversary of her death," Elena interrupts. "And of the day we left, and of the promise you made to Chuy and Lalo to come back. Lalo's even taking a day off at the clinic to come."

I think of all the people I won't, or can't, see. Lalo. Chuy. Elena. The nephew I've never held. Abuelita, Javi, and Moisés. There's no belonging—here or in San Jacinto or anywhere—without longing.

"*Y La Virgencita?*" Elena asks. Her voice has dropped to a whisper.

"She's staying here with me until I can cross *la línea* and come back again freely," I explain.

"Okay, Miguel." Elena's voice is almost inaudible now. "If it means you'll come someday, okay. *Te quiero mucho,* Miguel."

"I love you, too." I hang up the phone. We don't say good-bye. We never do.

The fog has moved in. It covers the whole bridge now, except for the very southern end. I'm going to walk all the way across the bridge today, because I've never done it, because I want to see what's there to the north, on the other side.

I put on my sweatshirt, zip it up tight, and look at myself in the mirror. There's the same old Miguel I was in San Jacinto, just a little taller, my face filled out some, a new moustache beginning to sprout. On the outside, the same me.

Inside, it's different. I thought I'd find the real Miguel, the one I thought I couldn't be in Mexico, once I crossed *la línea*. I didn't understand that there are thousands of *líneas* to cross in a life. Sometimes you see the border and you walk right across, eyes wide open. You know you will change. You know everything will be different.

Other times, you don't know you've crossed a border until you reach the other side. Until you turn, and look back at *la línea*, surprised.

Later I'll call Papá to let him know what I've decided to do next with my life. I'll tell him all about the next *línea* I'm planning to cross, and maybe the one after that.

ABOUT THIS BOOK

La Línea is the result of the fortunate convergence of my married and professional lives. This book would not have happened without both.

When my husband, Luis, and I met and fell in love in 1971, I was welcomed into his family. The Jaramillos have taught me a deep appreciation for the complex nature of Mexican families in the United States. They have shown me that there are many ways to be Mexican *and* American, culturally and linguistically. They also illustrate the different ways Americans of Mexican descent are citizens of this country.

Jaramillos have lived for many, many generations in New Mexico. My father-in-law, Lalo (Edward), liked to remind us, "We didn't come to the United States. The United States came to us." My mother-in-law, Tomasa, called Tommie, grew up in El Paso, Texas. Both her parents were immigrants from Mexico.

Luis and his five siblings were all born and raised in El Paso, right on the border. In fact, you can see the border from the family house. Lalo and Tommie never turned away anyone who came to the door, hungry and scared, straight from the other side of the Rio Grande.

While Luis became a lawyer, I became a middle school teacher. His career has been dedicated to seeking equal justice for migrant farmworkers and their families, most of whom are Mexican immigrants. Like my husband's clients, more than 95 percent of my students are Mexican in origin. Their parents work in the fields or packing sheds of the Salinas Valley. Some of my students were born in the United States; others immigrated in elementary or middle school.

La Línea is fiction, but it is based on real events.

The *mata gente* is real, although it is known by several different nicknames in Mexico. Migrants traveling through Mexico often hop trains as a way to get north, facing constant physical danger.

The Mexican government has established formal procedures to deter migration through Mexico and across its southern and northern borders.

People in *pueblitos* in Mexico, particularly in Veracruz, routinely throw food and other goods to migrants on the trains. These are humble communities whose residents care deeply about the plight of the migrants. They have few resources, but they give what they can.

Private American citizens, individually and in organized vigilante-type groups, patrol and enforce immigration on the U.S. side of the border.

Many immigrants lose their lives attempting to cross the border. In the Sonoran desert area of Arizona alone, several hundred die each year from dehydration, hypothermia, or violence. Thousands have died in the border area that stretches from California, across Arizona and New Mexico, to Texas.

Operation Gatekeeper was instituted by the U.S. Border Patrol in 1994 as a strategy to check the flow of immigrants at traditional border crossings. This effort has pushed immigrants to cross at increasingly remote, uninhabited, and dangerous parts of the border.

Humanitarian efforts save many, many lives at the border. Human rights, religious, and political organizations work tirelessly to safeguard immigrants.

Hundreds of thousands are apprehended and deported at the border each year, but just as many make it across. An unknown number are children and teenagers, with and without parents or relatives to help them. Most are willing to attempt the crossing multiple times.

The total number of undocumented people in the United States is estimated to be more than 10 million. Sixty percent are from Mexico, 20 percent are from Central America, and 20 percent are from Asia and other places.

Which takes me back to my own students. Many, many of my students have been and continue to be new-arrival immigrants, twelve, thirteen, fourteen years old. They set foot in my classroom not knowing a word of English, some having survived a journey that is daunting for even the hardiest of individuals. From them I have learned the meaning of optimism, courage, and determination.

This is their story. I wrote it for them.

ABOUT THE AUTHOR

Ann Jaramillo says, "I was working in my classroom one day after school when Maria asked if she could help me. A newly arrived immigrant from Mexico, thirteen years old and an eighth grader, she was smart and eager to learn English.

"At one point, Maria picked up the photo of my grown sons, Luis and Mateo, that sits on my desk. She wanted to know all about them, including if they had always lived with me. 'Why?' I asked, surprised by the question

"'My grandmother was my mother in Mexico,' Maria answered. 'When I came here, I didn't remember my mother. I hadn't seen her for years. I didn't even know her.'

"That conversation was the seed of this book. My students find very few books that reflect their lives and experiences. I was determined to write one that did."

Ann Jaramillo, who lives in Salinas, California, teaches English as a Second Language to seventh and eighth graders. This is her first book.

ANN JARAMILLO

What was your first job?
My first regular job, where I earned an hourly wage, was in a very small medical laboratory. My main duty was to rinse the gross stuff (dried, icky blood and smelly urine) out of test tubes before putting them in the sterilizer. The next job I had was for three summers in high school and college. I worked at a small, local frozen-food factory that processed and packaged peas and corn. Seven days a week, twelve hours a day, I "graded" peas: for every ton of peas that came down the chute, I had to actually peel fifty individual peas and plop them into a salt solution. I then counted how many sank! Since I did it thousands of times, I still remember that if three or fewer sink, the peas are Grade A. Neither of these jobs was interesting or challenging, but I learned a lot about how to persevere at something repetitive and mundane.

What did you want to be when you grew up?
I don't remember wanting to "be" anything in particular. I was more focused on things I wanted to "do." I looked up to people that I thought both made a difference in the world and led impossibly daring and (it seemed to me) romantic lives. Albert Schweitzer and Amelia Earhart come to mind,

and later, Cesar Chavez and Martin Luther King. I had no idea how to combine what I admired in people with my own real life (I didn't want to be either a doctor or an aviator). I didn't even know I was going to be a teacher, and that it was a perfect life's work for me, until I finished college and landed in a classroom.

Which of your characters is most like you?

It won't surprise you if I say I am most like Elena in *La Línea*, especially in one aspect: my persistence. There are other ways to think about this quality, of course! My family and best friends describe me as headstrong (a somewhat positive spin on this trait) or stubborn (not so flattering). Elena refuses to give up on her desire to go north with Miguel, to sometimes disastrous results. On the other hand, she is just as stubborn in her belief in Javi's goodness. I've learned that a character trait can be your best asset or your worst fault.

What's your idea of the best meal ever?

That's so hard, because I love almost all kinds of food and I love to cook. For sure, I'd make wild blackberry pie for dessert, with homemade crust, of course. Then, there would be fresh organic lettuce salad from our garden and baby green beans. And I'd have to have *mole oaxaqueno*, deep, dark, and full.

Which do you like better: cats or dogs?

I'm definitely a dog person. In fact, I'm crazy about dogs. We had a black lab, Ace, when I was growing up and a couple of German shorthairs, Fritz and Gretel. Because we lived in a rural place, the dogs were outside dogs and roamed around at will. They were part of our play and our talk. Ace would sprawl on top of our sleeping bags when we slept outside in the summer and we saw him as our protector. Dogs forgive your faults and comfort you when you're sad. They're faithful.

Where do you find inspiration for your writing?
My students and their families are my primary inspiration. Their lives are complicated and fascinating and full of stories waiting to be told. Most of them are newly arrived immigrant students from Mexico, and even though they hold some experiences in common, each has his or her own.

If you were stranded on a desert island, who would you want for company?
That's the easiest question of all. For sure, the one person I'd want with me is my husband, Luis Jaramillo. He's the kindest, most generous person I've ever known. He's also smart, funny, and handsome. We laugh, and cry, about the same things.

What's the best advice you have ever received about writing?
One time, in the midst of writing *La Línea*, I was really stuck about where to go next with the story. All of these questions kept rattling around in my head: What should/could happen? What would make sense for the characters to say/do? How can I make this part work with what came before and what will follow? It really stopped me from making progress. I complained to my son, Luis, who is also a writer. He said, "Mom, just write one bad paragraph after another. Keep writing. You can always throw it away or go back and fix or change it." It was great advice! There's nothing worse than writing nothing.